OTHER BOOKS BY EDIE RAMER

Contemporary
CHRISTMAS AT ANGEL LAKE (Rescued Hearts, book 2)
HEARTS IN MOTION (Rescued Hearts, # 1)
MUST WORSHIP CATS (a Miracle Interrupted novella)
STARDUST MIRACLE (a Miracle Interrupted novel)
MIRACLE LANE (a Miracle Interrupted novel)
MIRACLE PIE (a Miracle Interrupted novel)
MO'S HEART (a Miracle Interrupted novel)
YOU'VE GOT MURDER co-written with Karin Tabke

Paranormal
CATTITUDE
DEAD PEOPLE
DEAD PEOPLE IN LOVE (short story)
DRAGON BLUES

Science Fiction Romance
GALAXY GIRLS
MIXING IT UP (a Galaxy Girls novella)

Short Stories
The Fat Cat in ENTANGLED, a Paranormal Anthology
(all proceeds go to Breast Cancer Research Foundation)
The Kiss in EVERY WITCH WAY BUT WICKED
(all proceeds go to Kids Need to Read)

For updates, sign up for the Edie's newsletter at
www.edieramer.com.

HEARTS IN MOTION

Copyright © 2013 by Edie Ramer

All rights reserved by author

Cover design by Laura Morrigan

ISBN-13: ISBN: 978-1-939328-08-3

Hearts in Motion

Rescued Hearts, book 1

Edie Ramer

Blue Walrus Books

1

Abby Pimm knew every day mattered...but today mattered more. Panting from exertion and excitement, she lifted two pieces of cat furniture into the back of her SUV. After making sure they wouldn't fall, she dashed into the house to grab her tote and kiss each of the cats goodbye—her own two and her foster kitten. When she kissed her golden retriever, he returned the favor with a sloppy, smelly tongue swipe on her chin.

"I'll be back soon," she said. "And everything will be all right for us."

Then she raced to the SUV, jumped in, and fired up the engine, thinking that everything *had* to be all right.

Anything could happen today, good or bad, and this was one time she'd better not screw anything up.

———

Are we going to starve? Epic, the white kitten who was too small and too thin and too nervous, asked. She was backed up to the couch, ready to dart behind it. *Is she going to come back? Is she going to forget about us?*

Perched on top of the wall-climbing cat ladder, Quigley made an impatient mewl. He was young and sleek and adventuresome, his black fur shining. He'd been brought to Mom for fostering as a newborn with his mom and his two brothers. When he wasn't adopted after a month, Mom had kept him, and he only knew the comfort of Mom's home. The assurance that he was loved.

Minnie tilted her head and her ears. She was the oldest and the one who knew the world the best.

Outside of their home, it was a bad place. A very bad place.

Cars tried to run you over.

Mean dogs tried to bite you.

People yelled at you.

She was alive today because Mom had saved her. Mom had run into traffic and scooped her up when she'd been too small and weak to squirm away. She'd cried over her as she'd taken her into her car. She'd cried all the way home. She'd fed her tuna, and she'd given her water.

And most of all, she'd loved her.

"I'll take care of you," she'd whispered. "You're my kitten now, and I won't let anything bad happen to you."

It was a long time ago, long before Quigley came to live with them, but Minnie had never forgotten.

Mom would never let us starve, Minnie said.

Don't worry about Mom going away, Lion the big, goofy dog said. *If any bad people come, I'll protect you.*

Quigley flicked his tail. *Lion will lick the bad people to death.*

I like people, Lion said. *And they like me.*

Minnie leaped up to her seat on the windowsill and looked outside. Mom would figure out a way to take care of them. Mom always did. For a human, she was small. But cats knew it wasn't the inches that counted.

Mom's almost as smart as me, she said.

Lion lifted his head. *And almost as loving as me.*

But she can't jump like me, Quigley bragged then took a flying leap to the couch.

Maybe not, Lion said, *but she's the one who feeds you.*

The kitten made a distressed cry. Minnie gave Lion and Quigley a sharp look then turned her back on them, jumped to the floor, and padded over to Epic to rub her chin on the small head.

Lion climbed onto the couch, where he wasn't allowed when Mom was home. He curled up to sleep.

Not a bad idea. *I know what we should do,* Minnie said to Epic, who peered up at her with big eyes, not saying anything.

What? Quigley asked.

Sleep. She jumped on the couch, on the other end from Lion. Two of the walls had trees with perches built for them, but they weren't big enough for cuddling. She glanced down at Epic. *Can you jump up?*

Epic hopped up. Fell. Hopped up again. Fell. The next time she stared for a moment before doing it the right way, taking into account the muscle power needed for the distance. Then her back legs bent...and she sprang up, landing next to Minnie and squeaking her surprise that she'd made it.

Minnie stretched out and the kitten settled next to her, her body quaking. Minnie put her front paws around Epic. A movement on the couch told Minnie that Quigley was settling down, too.

Mom will fix everything. Minnie patted the side of Epic's face. *Everything will be all right.*

And if Mom couldn't do it herself, they would have to

help her. Somehow.

Epic stopped trembling, her body relaxing, her soft breaths even with sleep. Minnie pressed her face against the back of the kitten's head. Right now a sunbeam formed a large rectangle of light on the couch, she was surrounded by warm bodies, her tummy was full, and she was going to do what all cats did during times like this.

Close her eyes and nap.

———

Lion greeted Abby at the back door. She dropped to her knees and hugged him, holding on tightly, needing his steady warmth and caring. He pushed the side of his head against her neck, as if he knew she needed comforting.

Sometimes she thought she screwed up everything she touched.

Her sister's life was so different from Abby's at the same age. Abby had had more clothes, more money, more house, more security...more love.

It wasn't all her fault, but that didn't take away the tight knot of failure in her gut.

Right now only money would untie that knot.

"Oh, you sweet boy." Her voice came out choked. "I love you."

In the hall behind him, Quigley and Minnie stared at her, though they usually napped during midday. It felt to Abby as if they knew how important the meeting had been.

As if they knew she hadn't been able to convince the

two women and three men to finance her start-up company.

That was crazy thinking. There was no way they could know.

She sniffed in her tears, dropped a kiss on Lion's head, then rose to her feet. She smiled at the cats even though her cheek muscles hurt.

"One door closed," she said, practicing for when Grace came home from school. "But it's all right." She straightened her shoulders and set her jaw, feeling her eyes burn and her determination rise.

She reminded herself of all the others before her who'd failed but kept going until they made it. Reminded herself of the old saying that the only real failures were the ones who gave up.

Besides, there was still the one way they could keep going. It was a way she hated, but she would not allow this defeat to stop her. She would *not* give up.

"There will be another door." This time the words rang out.

Quigley made an odd growling sound.

"And when I find it, do you know what I'm going to do?"

They both stared at her.

"Whatever it takes to walk through it." She was tired of failure. Sick to her stomach of it. She needed to succeed for Grace, for her business partner, for her cats, for her dog...and for herself.

She clenched her hands into fists. Pouring passion and determination into her voice, she added, "Even if I need to take an axe to it."

2

Two weeks. Just two weeks.

In his aunt Daisy's colorful condo, Holden Ramsay determined he would make everything work in the next two weeks.

Make it work for the 435 employees who were employed by his company.

And maybe more important, for the blond six-year-old with the sad blue eyes who was gaping at the zigzag wood sculpture/cat ladder/bookcase that took up one wall of Daisy's living room.

"They dropped her off at your house and *ran*?" Daisy asked in what for her was a low voice, not seeming to notice how her voice carried.

Seated on a blue-striped chair, Holden Ramsay glanced at the small child who didn't look anything like him. She didn't appear to have heard his aunt, her head tilted up as she stared at the brown tabby curled on the top perch.

He glanced back to his aunt Daisy, sitting on her lime-green sofa, and he recalled when he was a child and her apartment had reminded him of an ice cream shop in a picture book. In most ways she was still the energetic aunt who'd scooped him out of his grandparents' dreary home once a week when he was a kid, promising to take him somewhere fun. But though her backbone was as stiff as ever, her hair was pure white now instead of dark brown like his, and the skin on her pronounced Ramsay chin sagged a bit.

He'd aged, too. Thirty-two, though for the past three years he'd been written up in the business pages as "the young CEO and president of Eagleton Furniture." Sometimes Holden felt as if the business weighed him down like the world on Atlas's shoulders.

"I don't want to talk about her grandparents," he said. Not here, where the girl might overhear. He'd told Daisy the bare bones on the phone before he and Cara had driven over. How his ex's parents had dropped the girl off at his house at nine last night, informed him that their daughter had flown to Europe with her new lover who didn't want kids around, and the girl's nanny had stolen from them—the umpteenth nanny that hadn't worked out—and it was about time he took care of his own child.

His own child.

If she had been his child, he would never have let Juliana take her away.

At the time, he was doing Juliana a favor, letting her parents believe he was Cara's father in return for an uncontested divorce. But as soon as he talked to Juliana, that had to change.

"Juliana's parents said she would be back in two weeks," he said. "This will be over soon."

"And then what?"

Images ran through his mind of the night before. Night hadn't quite fallen, the sky the color of dusk—the time of day when things didn't appear quite real, even with the lights on his front door and the garage illuminating the driveway of his lakeside home. Maybe that's what had made his former father-in-law, a husky Palm Beach real estate broker who prided himself on sealing the deal, pick the girl up and thrust her into his chest.

Holden had automatically grabbed her before she fell onto the hard concrete of the front porch.

And while he'd held the lost little girl, he'd felt her quivering, felt her pure fear.

Though his younger brother often said Holden had a heart like a hardball, he did have one, and it wouldn't let him drop the girl and race after his former in-laws as they scurried to the taxi, his former mother-in-law leaving a suitcase on the driveway. Both of them in a hurry to escape and catch the first flight back to their Palm Springs home, their country club, and their cocktail parties. To play golf and have lunch and gossip about friends.

A small child didn't fit in to that lifestyle.

"I let them go," he said, hearing the steel in his voice. "I'll have to get ahold of Juliana. I put a call out to a couple mutual friends for her phone number. In the meantime, I thought I could put the girl in daycare."

"Darling, I'm not a daycare. Why here?"

"I took the girl to a place this morning. She started shaking when we walked in the place and she saw all the kids in the hall. She's not used to other children. From what she's said, Juliana wasn't around much, and her grandparents kept her at their home, with revolving nannies taking care of her. There weren't opportunities for her to meet other kids."

He glanced at the girl again. *Cara.* He needed to

remember to call her by her name. Not *the girl*. After all, he'd given it to her in the hospital.

How ironic, him naming her.

And damn Juliana for being as careless a mother as she'd been a wife. Taking off and leaving the child alone so often. Just like his parents had done to him. They lived in Cannes now, and he hadn't seen them for four years.

And Juliana's parents...double damn then. Two of the most selfish and cold people he'd met.

At least his grandfather had had passion, even if it had been directed at his business.

"She likes Elvis." His aunt nodded her chin at the wood sculpture. Her black and white cat had jumped down to the first perch, his head raised to inspect the girl. Cara was bending down, holding out her hand, the cat's nose pointed up to sniff her.

"Elvis seems to reciprocate the emotion." He looked back at his aunt. "It's just two short weeks. If you—"

"Darling," she said, "I'm meeting a friend for lunch today. Tomorrow I have a doctor's appointment. Just a check-up, but I don't want to miss it, and she would be bored silly waiting for me. Plus, I have lunch with friends on Thursday. On Saturday, I'm meeting with my book club, and on Sunday, I'm going to a play in Madison. Besides, what makes you think the girl is better off with me than the grandparents?"

"You wouldn't leave her with a nanny all day, every day. Even my grandparents didn't do that."

"That's because my parents were too stingy to pay for a nanny," she said.

He laughed. Too true about his stern grandparents. Despite the fact that they were one of the wealthiest families in Eagleton, his grandmother had made breakfast for him every day and sent him off to school herself. No private school for him or his brother. And every night, his grandfather had checked their homework to make sure they'd done it.

They'd ruined his father, his grandmother had said often. They weren't doing the same thing with him and Ryan.

"Cara needs someone younger than me," Daisy said. "Someone lively, who will do things with her."

"I hope you're not talking about Portia. She has her own career. I won't ask her to stop it for me."

"Of course I'm not thinking of Portia." Daisy made a gesture with her hand, as if swatting away a fly. "Didn't I say someone lively?"

He stared at her, not saying anything, while she gazed blandly back at him, her lips quivering with silent laughter.

A stalemate. But in his mind, he was winning. Portia's tranquility—or lack of vivacity, his aunt would say—was what had drawn him to her. Portia was a calm lake where Juliana had been a frenetic lightning storm.

"You have someone lively in mind?" he asked, hoping it wasn't someone too lively. The last thing Cara needed in her life was a clone of her mother.

Daisy beamed. "The girl who makes my cat furniture. She works from home, and—"

"Whoa." He got to his feet. "Saws and woodworking tools aren't a safe place for a small child."

"You're a good man." Daisy stood and reached out to pat his cheek. "Abby does the designing and the marketing. She's the people person. Her partner does the woodwork."

"Partner as in a live-in lover?"

"You're such a prude." With her face animated and her eyes bright, Daisy still looked like the fun aunt from his youth, with only a few more wrinkles, a few more pounds, and a change of hair color. "Her partner is a woman and, no, she doesn't live with Abby."

"How do you know them so well?"

"Abby fosters cats. Elvis was staying with her when I adopted him. And then I realized I knew her parents. Not well, but we were acquaintances."

"The...thing on your wall. That's one of hers?"

She twisted to smile at it before twisting back. "Beautiful, isn't it? I admire their work and their ambition."

"What about kids? Does she have anyone for Cara to play with?"

"Her sister is fourteen. I think she has summer school so won't be home for at least part of the day. Their parents died nine years ago. Their father was a neurosurgeon, and their mother was a chef. Abby quit college to raise her sister. She's doing a wonderful job. They're both amazing young women."

He stared at her for a long moment as a memory lit in his mind of a girl-woman with red hair who'd made him laugh years ago when he was going to college.

"*Abby,*" she'd said. "*My name is Abby.*"

He blinked the image away.

"You're not fixing me up, are you?" he asked.

"Of course not. You're engaged." Her lips curved into a smirk. "Besides, you wouldn't do for Abby. She's like...a bright, shining star. While you're..."

"A dark cloud?" he asked.

She laughed again. "Not quite, dear. But you're too solid for her. It would be an awful match. Like putting together a butterfly and a toad."

"Obviously I'm not the butterfly."

"You would hate being a butterfly. You'd rather be the toad. The king of your own lily pad." She beamed at him. "You know I love you, darling."

"Despite my faults."

"Everyone has faults."

"Except you."

"Especially me. I'm selfish. I enjoy my little luxuries." She swept her hand out to encompass her jewelry-box-like condo. "And I'm fond of getting my own way. The reason I never married."

His cell phone buzzed. He took it from his belt and saw a text from his secretary. "I have an appointment in a half hour. It's important."

"Cara's important, too."

"That's why I want to leave her with you. Someone I trust." He took her right hand in both of his, leaning close to look into her eyes. "What I'm doing isn't as important to me as it is to all the employees at Eagleton Furniture. Every year it gets harder to compete against the cheaper furniture coming from Asia. I could retire tomorrow, and everyone in the family would live a life of ease. Not them." He released her hand and stepped back.

"Some would be okay. They might even make better lives for themselves. But others..."

Frown lines on her forehead deepened. "Life is always so serious for you."

"Life is serious when you have so much power over people's lives. If I don't do my job well, they'll lose theirs. And it's not just jobs, it's insurance, too. Many of the employees have been with us for a long time. You can't deny there's age discrimination. The older workers would have a hard time finding a new job. They or their dependents might have health problems. To some, it might make a difference between a quality life and barely getting by. To others, it might mean life or death."

She sighed. "I wish you were exaggerating."

"I wish I were, too."

"You said you trusted me. Do you mean it?"

"Absolutely." But a twinge of worry twisted inside him....

"Then I'll do what's best for Cara." She made a shooing motion. "You run off to your business. Save the world in your own little way."

"Like a superhero," he said.

"You keep telling yourself that." Her eyes gleamed with humor. "While you're saving the world, I'll take Cara to Abby's and make her an offer she can't resist."

"What kind of offer?"

Her eyebrows rose. "You said you trusted me. Just go. You won't be sorry."

Every time someone said he wouldn't be sorry, he usually was. But he nodded and turned to Cara to tell her he was leaving her with someone she'd just met. As if she were a package that was being handed from one person to another.

She looked up at him, her eyes blank, and he did something he hadn't planned on doing. He went to her, crouched, and hugged her. She stood stiff, as if unused to hugs or any shows of affection.

"I'll be back," he said. And then he left, his strides fast.

He would be glad when these two weeks were over.

3

Abby watched Holden Ramsay stride up her front sidewalk, purpose in every firm step. Daisy had told her he was coming to pick up Cara and, in the future, would be dropping her off in the mornings. If not for the girl's sad little face, she might have smiled at Daisy and made her apologies.

That and the fact that she desperately needed the money. Daisy's proposal was an answer to the prayer she hadn't made. Enough to pay a few bills and get them over this hump.

Only two weeks...

By then she would think of something to keep them going. Something to save them all.

She crossed her arms and leaned against the doorjamb.

He hadn't changed. A face like that could be on a movie poster. A chin that looked stubborn. A line permanently etched into his forehead. Brows slashed above silvery-blue eyes that made her feel as if he were peering into her soul.

"Well, if it isn't the Big Bad Wolf at my door," she said.

His face that had been set in hard lines made a lightning change to surprise. The lower half of his face opened into a grin, and she thought it was like watching a large rock crack in half.

Still looking at him, she amended that to a very handsome rock.

"Do you really want me to say the Big Bad Wolf's reply, Little Red?"

She groaned, though she'd asked for it. When would she learn to keep her mouth shut? So what if keeping her mouth shut was boring? She could be boring.

But not today.

She pushed away from the doorjamb. "Only if you want to get your shin kicked."

"Hard to resist that line. I could take my chances."

"And I could kick higher."

He laughed again and shook his head. "You have an odd effect on me."

"Join the crowd." She gestured behind him, as if hundreds of confused, invisible people were milling there, afraid to get too close to her. "So you are human. That's not what I've been hearing."

"I'm sure it's nothing Ryan ever said about me."

"It was a long time ago that I dated your brother for a glorious ten days." She rolled her eyes, though there was a small ache in her chest. Not for Ryan. For her parents, who'd laughed at her when she'd fumed at them about Ryan and his brother, until she'd laughed, too.

She tamped the ache down. She preferred to think they were still alive somewhere, in another dimension, another place. Maybe just a breath away, sending her and Grace love. Telling her they believed in her. Telling her not to let one of the city's wealthiest bachelors overwhelm her.

As if.

"My brother's an asshole," he said.

"No arguments." She grinned. "You said the same thing nine years ago when I went to your house and asked for my physics book back."

"Demanded it back. Said you were going to call the police on Ryan if I didn't get it for you." He lowered his head to peer down at her, reminding her that her feet were bare, and she was about ten inches shorter than his six-foot-or-more height.

She straightened her spine. "And you told me to go ahead and call the police."

He chuckled.

"You got the book for me anyway."

"I was afraid you would combust in my grandmother's foyer if I didn't. How did you do in physics, anyway?"

She opened the screen door. "Like I said, a long time ago. Come on in."

From the way his smile dropped, she guessed he remembered her parents had died in the accident less than two weeks after her visit to his grandparents' house. *Don't pity me.*

If he did, she might kick him in the shins, after all.

Laughter came from the back, two voices mingling. Grace's, soft and low, joined with Cara's higher, younger laugh that pitched up and down. As if she didn't laugh often and was unsure how to do it.

Abby's sense of goodwill dissipated, and she glared at him. This was his *daughter*. How could he have allowed her life to be so joyless?

"Your daughter is a sweetheart. We fed her dinner

already. Daisy didn't know if she had allergies, but Cara said she didn't, so I fed her a spinach salad with strawberries and nuts for lunch. For dinner, we had chicken stir-fry."

He stepped inside her living room, his expression shuttering, and now he finally looked like the stern businessman he was known to be. The Big Bad Wolf indeed. "Sounds fine," he said, no inflection in his voice.

She rushed ahead of him, leading the way to Grace's bedroom, where the two girls were playing. This had been a perfect June day, and Abby had managed to enjoy it despite all the thoughts whirling in her head. The worries, the plans, the dream so close to fruition, if only she could get someone to back her.

Not this man, though. He couldn't even take care of the daughter he'd only seen twice in his life.

Not his fault, Daisy had said.

He was Cara's father. If not his fault, whose?

But she hadn't asked then and wasn't asking now. She would just try to make Cara happy for the short time she was with them, the same as she did for the rescue cats.

"You can't change the world," her father used to say. "You can just do your part to make it better."

She'd feel happier about it if she didn't have to do her part two or three times—sometimes more—before she got it right.

She led Holden down the hall of the small, one-story house, with the two bedrooms and the tiny third one she used for her office. The front of the house with the open kitchen and living room felt bigger because of the way the rooms flowed, but she'd learned that more than two foster cats were too many.

Cara didn't take up much more space than a kitten.

Not like the man behind her. His presence seemed to fill the house.

They reached the bedroom, and she saw the three cats, one dog, and the two girls sitting on the carpet. The white cat reacted first, leaping out of Cara's arms and dashing beneath the bed.

On the blue bedspread that matched her Siamese eyes, Minnie sat in the middle of the bed and watched them, waiting to see what would happen next. Quigley, her beautiful black with the shining fur, leaped down from the dresser to race ahead of Lion, her gorgeous golden retriever, and weave around her ankles.

With their high range of hearing, the cats and the dog had heard them heading to the bedroom. Abby thought it was a testament to the foster cat's trust in her and Grace that she'd waited for Holden's entry into the room before she ran and hid.

Cara stared at her father, her giggle stopped. She looked as if she'd like to crawl under the bed after Epic.

Sadness filled Abby to see that the girl felt safer with the cats and dog than her father. Abby petted Quigley and Lion then stepped inside the room and knelt in front of Cara. "I had fun with you today, but your dad is here now. You have to go home for the night."

Cara nodded, her eyes down. It had taken two hours for Abby to get more than a few words out of the small girl. Her first full sentence had been to Lion and then Minnie, who'd regally allowed the girl to pet her. And when Cara had lifted the white kitten to her chest, Abby could've sworn she'd heard both girl and kitten purr.

Sometimes love happened that way.

And then Grace had returned from summer school and had taken over entertaining while Abby crafted carpet-covered pads for the cat furniture. When she wasn't using the staple gun, she could hear Grace talking, and after a while, Cara's small voice replying. Cara had been unable to resist Grace's quiet charm any more than the teen boys who kept showing up at their house at inconvenient times.

"We'll see you tomorrow," Abby said. "Lion and the kittens and me. We'll have a good time."

Cara nodded, giving her a shy smile. Abby beamed at her, hugged her, then stood and held out her hand. Cara put her little hand in hers, and Abby pulled her to her feet.

"Now you can go back home with your daddy," Abby said. And she finally glanced up at his stunned face.

She held Cara's hand to him to take. He moved in slow motion, and when Abby let go of Cara, for a second his hand hovered above Cara's until his fingers clasped hers. He and she stared at each other for another moment, and the air was silent except for everyone's breathing.

Grace got to her feet, and the odd hush shattered. Abby introduced her to Holden then pointed out the cats and Lion by name. He told her he'd always admired Siamese. As he talked, he kept glancing down at his hand holding Cara's.

Finally he said they had to leave and told Cara to say goodbye.

But she didn't. Locked into silence already, she gave Abby and Grace a scared glance.

Abby wanted to snatch her back. She speared Holden with a look that should have razed him to the ground like the cretin he was. But he was staring at Cara, and on his too handsome face, she saw worry and helplessness.

The next second, it was gone, and he and Cara headed to the hallway. Abby and Grace followed them to the front door, Lion padding behind them, the two cats darting ahead. In the living room, Abby wished Holden and Cara a good night. She and Grace stayed at the front door and watched him put Cara into a child's car seat in the back of a Ford hybrid.

Some of the tension seeped out of her tight muscles.

It was going to be okay, she thought, and realized that, though he might be the richest man in Eagleton, for a moment, she'd felt sorry for him.

When she turned, Grace hugged her. "I'm glad I have you," Grace said. "You're the best."

Abby hugged her tightly. She wasn't the best and had screwed up a couple hundred times—maybe a couple thousand—but at least she'd always loved Grace. That was one thing Grace had never doubted.

"No, you're the best." She pulled back. "You know what we should do tonight?"

"Homework?" Grace pulled a face.

Abby laughed. "Let's watch DVDs of Mom and Dad."

———

Mom and Grace had been watching the pictures on TV for a long time when Lion got to his feet. *They're crying. We need to go to them.*

It's a happy cry, Minnie said patiently. No matter how often she told Lion this, he didn't understand the difference. It was true that dogs weren't as smart as cats, though on the whole, she found Lion sensible. He did defer to her knowledge and years. Something Quigley didn't do as often as she liked. *They're watching movies of their mom and dad.*

I'd like to see their mom and dad, Epic said.

You can't, Quigley said, *they're in heaven.*

What's heaven? Epic asked.

Minnie leveled her now-you've-done-it glare on Quigley before turning to the little one. *That's where cats go to play after they leave earth. Cats and their people.*

And dogs, Lion said.

Special dogs, Minnie said.

I don't want to go there unless Mom and Grace can go, too. Quigley leaped to the floor.

So they can feed you, Minnie said.

Yes. Quigley twisted his head all the way around to give her an approving look. Sarcasm was a special cat talent that usually zipped right over his shiny black head.

Will Mom be able to feed us now? Epic asked.

Quigley made a huffing sound. *Of course. That's why we're taking care of the girl. So you better be nice to her.*

I like her, Epic said. *Maybe I can live with her.*

Minnie was shooting Quigley a look to stop him from saying anything mean when an extra loud sob came to her ear. Grace. Lion was the first to his feet, hurrying to her, but Quigley dashed past him.

Though Minnie was older, she was still in her prime.

She leaped off the table, landing close to the girl and woman stretched out on the floor.

Lion and Quigley snuggled on either side of Grace. Minnie rubbed her mouth against Grace's chin, nose, and jaw to make her feel better.

Because making Mom and Grace feel better was their job.

Protecting their house from vermin was their job.

And most of all, giving humans love was their job.

A hand curved over Minnie's head, and fingers found the just-right spot to massage behind her ear. *Mom.* Minnie purred, her throat and chest vibrating. She closed her eyes and felt the urge to knead with her paws while Mom did her job: giving love back.

Sometimes Minnie thought cat heaven couldn't be better than life with Mom and Grace. Minnie had heard Mom say on the phone that with Cara in their house during the sunlight hours, they'd been given a reprieve from being thrown out in the street.

Mom had laughed, but it was a laugh that wasn't funny.

Being thrown out in the street wasn't in any way funny for Minnie, either. Bad things were in the street. Bad people who liked to hurt small animals.

There had to be some way to stay here. Not for a short time. Forever.

She started kneading the carpet. She would have to think on it.

4

"It was a hard day for me, too." Portia sipped her favorite chardonnay. As usual, her complexion was flawless, her face a perfect oval, her shiny, dark hair short, in a boy's cut, but she pulled it off. They sat in the built-in dining set of his stark gray and cream kitchen that overlooked Angel Lake.

She looked like she belonged in this place, Holden thought. Elegant and sleek. Whereas Abby would be an incongruity. The only brightly colored decoration on a silver and pale-blue-decorated Christmas tree.

Not that there was any reason for Abby to be in his house, though he could easily imagine her in his bed. Naked. That laughing smile on her face, her red-gold hair spread over his pillow. Her arms out to—

He shut off his thoughts. Too inappropriate.

A glance at Portia cooled his inappropriate libido.

"I had to give a family distressing news about their child's health," Portia continued, her calm expression unchanging, talking about her job as a genetic counselor at Eagleton Community Hospital. "And I passed on bad news about the paternity of a child. The woman's husband was devastated."

Not answering, Holden took a sip of his brandy, thinking about Cara, his gut twisting.

If his ex had been faithful, Cara could have been his. Instead, she was a quiet little ghost who was making a big stir in his nerves and his life.

A child was a responsibility, one he wasn't ready for. He had to stop himself from getting up and looking in on her to make sure she was okay. She'd been sleeping when he'd checked on her an hour ago. He'd left the hall light on, the door open a crack. If she woke up, she could easily find him.

"The baby looked so much like the husband, too." Portia leaned forward. "The wife's parents belong to the country club, and they knew I was testing the DNA. The mother tried to bribe me to tell him the baby was his. For the child's sake, she said. Not because they were afraid for the marriage."

Her dry tone suggested she didn't believe the mother, and Holden made a sound of sympathy and agreement. This wasn't a topic he wanted to continue.

"She thought it would be like a poison in him."

His hand tightened on the cool glass, and he set it on the table before he shattered it with his grip.

"Of course, I said no," she continued. "The truth is always better."

"For the parent. Not necessarily the child."

"I have to disagree." Her voice stiffened. "This isn't something I do lightly. I believe it's better for the child to know the truth when he's young. If told correctly and without drama, it shouldn't be traumatic."

"In a perfect world," he said, coldness stabbing down his spine.

She leaned toward him. "I would *never* tell Cara the truth, if that's a concern. Though it's my professional opinion that falsehoods like this are confusing and unnecessary. If your ex-wife had told her parents the truth, they would never have dropped her off at your house."

He frowned, aware that she was right...but also aware that there were different degrees of truth. "I had Cara's...father investigated. The only reason he'd agree to take Cara would be for money."

"That's unfortunate." She put her long-fingered, slender hand atop of his. "I admire you for taking responsibility for the girl though she's not a blood relative. And when you consider the turmoil her mother put you through, it could be construed to be noble."

"My time with Juliana wasn't the best part of my life." *A living hell.* "But it's over, and I learned a valuable lesson."

"What was that?"

He smiled at her, an effort, because he didn't have the words to tell her that he'd decided his next life partner would fit all the priorities on his list: cool, serene, smart, responsible, educated, and financially secure enough not to need his money.

An image of Abby naked in his bed burned in his mind again.

He wiped it out. He'd made one colossal mistake following his libido. He wasn't doing it again. Instead, he directed his focus on his fiancée. "To wait for a woman as wonderful as you."

She tightened her hand around his, and the muscles in her face tightened, too, like a ripple in a calm pond. "We do seem to be in sync with one another." Relaxing her grip, she leaned back. "I'm glad you found someone dependable to take care of Cara. I remember meeting

Abby at hospital events. I went to her parents' funeral with my father." She frowned slightly then shrugged. "She was so...emotional. Her father was head of Neurology at Eagleton General. It's a shame someone with such promise and brilliance died so young. I'm sure her father had much to contribute to the world."

A chill crept up his spine. Her words were in praise of Abby's father as a physician. Maybe to Eagleton, Wisconsin, the father's contributions in the medical field were the finest things about his life. But knowing the daughter, with her vitality and passion, he suspected the father's finest achievements resided in a small house in Eagleton, Wisconsin.

"It's too bad he wasn't as brilliant when it came to money." Portia shook her head. "I heard there was hardly anything left for his daughters."

Holden frowned and thought of Cara. She wasn't his biological daughter, but it wouldn't hurt him to set something up for her. He doubted her mother would do it.

"I have another connection with Abby," Portia continued. "She's a partner in an enterprise with a sorority sister. Sam dropped out before med school. It's a shame. She was so promising." She shook her head, her lips pursed in disapproval. "And now she makes cat furniture. What a waste of brain power."

"Sam as in Samantha?" he asked.

She nodded. "Perhaps I'll call her. I read about their venture in a sorority newsletter. Sam and I roomed together for two years. I should ask if there's anything I can do."

"If she's anything like her partner, she'll tell you to adopt a kitten."

Portia's laugh was as smooth as the wine she'd been drinking. She brought up the napkin to pat her lips then stood in one graceful movement. "I should leave. I have another full day tomorrow, and I planned on looking over my notes tonight. Will this..."—she waved her hand toward the bedrooms in the back of the house—"change our plans for the weekend?"

He wiped his hand over his face, remembering they were going to a new exhibition at the art museum on Saturday then to a play on Sunday.

"Never mind." Her cool fingertips touched his wrist. "Of course you have to stay with Cara. The child comes first."

"It's just two weeks, and then I'll get my life back."

"Then you can concentrate on what's important," she said. "Your company."

He got to his feet. "The company won't wait until then. I concentrate on it every day."

She made a moue of sympathy and turned toward the door. Before leaving, they kissed without passion then separated. Sundown was coming soon, the daylight thinned to a pale gray, and as he watched her walk to her car, the thought came to him that she blended into the coming of the night. As if this time of shadows was her time.

He watched until she got in the car and backed out of his driveway. Only then did he head to the bedrooms, his strides lengthening. The girl should be sleeping, but he'd felt uneasy the entire time he'd been eating and talking, and now his uneasiness was getting more intense.

He started to run....

———————

Abby's mind was too busy for her to concentrate, her thoughts refusing to shut off, not allowing her to get lost in the romance she hadn't wanted to put down yesterday. Holding the book, she sat in the recliner that had belonged to her father. Minnie was inches from her elbow, on the top perch of the Double Seater, their biggest seller that came complete with a scratching pad. Epic was curled up on the perch below Minnie. Lion lay on his dog bed on the other side of the chair.

From the bedroom came Grace's voice, either on the phone or Skyping with one of her friends. Quigley must be with her.

Abby gazed at Minnie, whose blue eyes were open, staring at her as if she knew this would happen. "Something isn't adding up."

Minnie responded, her sentences long and with great inflexion and emotion.

Abby leaned toward her, as if Minnie were speaking a foreign language that her brain was too stupid and slow to understand. And if she could only understand, glorious secrets of the universe would open up for her.

At least, enough to get her life together. Right now, she'd take help wherever she could get it.

Which made her think of *him* again.

"You're right," she said. And Minnie made a sound that was half huff, half agreement. "My kitty sense is telling me something's wrong, too, and I'd better find out what's really going on."

She lowered the recliner's leg rest and pushed off from the seat, leaving her book behind. Her cell phone was on the ottoman. She grabbed it, found the number she wanted. The ring trilled four times on the other end, and she was expecting a robotic voice message when Daisy called out a greeting and asked if everything had gone okay.

"Did you see Cara?" Abby demanded. She wasn't in the mood to play nice. She felt as if she'd been tricked.

"Yes." Daisy's tone was cautious, and she was a woman who normally boomed out her words, confirming Abby's suspicions.

"She's like some cats I've fostered. Not used to being...cared for. I don't mean physically," she said quickly. "But as if they'd always been treated as a duty and a nuisance instead of precious and loved."

"Her mother had custody. Holden had no idea she was being neglected emotionally."

"That's what bothers me. He's the girl's father. Why wasn't he aware?"

"You should direct these questions to him."

"You think he'll answer?"

"I think he'll say it's none of your business."

"Like that's going to stop me."

"I should have known you'd be this way." Daisy laughed then abruptly stopped. "It was part of the divorce agreement. Lawyer shenanigans. Will you accept that and leave it alone?"

"If I believed that, I would. I don't know Holden well, but what I do know is that he isn't a man who would ignore his daughter. Maybe he isn't the warmest man in the world—"

A snort of laughter came over the phone.

"But he would feel responsible for her. At the least, he would visit her. And if he'd found her the way she is, so timid and...almost frightened, he would do whatever it took to make it right."

Daisy didn't say anything. Just silence came from the other end of the phone. This from a woman who, even if she didn't have the answer, always had an opinion.

"What? I'm right, aren't I?"

"How often have you met my nephew?" Daisy asked.

"Twice."

"And you know him that well?"

Abby frowned, feeling an itch inside her that she didn't like and didn't know how to scratch. "I don't know what you're getting at, but don't read anything into it. I'm a good judge of character."

Another half snort came over the phone. "Abby, I've met a couple of your boyfriends."

"They weren't awful."

"They were eye candy."

"What's wrong with that?" Abby felt defensive. She didn't go out that often, too busy being a mom as well as a big sister, taking Grace to dance lessons, soccer practice, track practice, swim lessons, sleepovers.... Cooking and cleaning and trying to be make enough money to pay for everything. And then there were the cats she fostered.

She'd been leading the life of a single mom when she was still a teenager. So when she did go out, why not flirt with the cute guys? Why not dance and have a good time?

Perhaps too good of a time.

When her parents had died, she'd been young and grieving, and sometimes she had gone a little crazy.

The crazy was mostly gone now, the grief still there but a hum now, no longer a rap song that kept shouting at her to get it while she could. Now she was concentrating on a future for Grace and herself—the future she'd silently promised her mom and dad nine years ago as she'd emptied their ashes into Angel Lake.

"Nothing wrong at all," Daisy said, bringing her back to the phone call. "I've had my share of eye candy."

"You were trying to change the subject from your nephew, weren't you?"

"It's not my subject to change." The laughter left Daisy's voice. "If you want to know more, you'll have to ask Holden."

"He'll give me one of his looks."

Daisy's laughter flowed. "For someone who's only spoken to him twice, you appear to know him very well."

Abby shrugged, though Daisy couldn't see her. "Aren't all men alike?"

"You darling girl, men are like cats. None of them are the same—not even in the dark." Her voice lowered. "Ask him, Abby. I dare you."

Then the line went dead.

"Daisy?" Abby said. "Daisy!"

Silence answered her. Abby clicked her phone off and set it down. Daisy had done that on purpose, ending it as she had. The older woman knew her too well. Knew just how hard it was for her to resist a dare....

———————

Holden opened the door, and the light from the hall spilled in. Cara lay on her stomach with the thin blanket pulled up to her shoulders, making small, hiccupping sobs. Almost silent, but each sob sliced through him like a crosscut saw. He stepped inside, and she stopped crying, becoming still. He had the idea that she was wishing she were invisible. That she was wishing he would step back into the hall and leave her.

"Cara?" He headed toward her. "Are you all right?"

Nothing. He could hear the hum of the house. The crickets singing. He even heard the slight breeze, the rustle of leaves from the birch tree outside her open window.

A shuddering exhale came from the bed, her held-in breath released. He knelt to be level with her. "Do you want anything to eat?"

She shook her head.

"A drink of water? Warm milk?"

She shook her head.

"Do you want me to tell you a story?"

She shook her head.

"I can't leave when you're crying. Will you tell me what's wrong?"

She didn't say anything, but another sob came. He had a strange urge to pick her up and hold her. To pat her back and tell her everything was going to be all right.

But he held back, his hands at his side. If he did that, she'd be more frightened than comforted. He was a stranger to her. And when the two weeks were up, she would go back to her mother or grandparents. Back to the same loveless life.

He straightened and glanced around the room and saw the chair in the corner. A compact, bedroom type, easy to lift. He took three strides to it then carried it back to her side. She'd turned her face to watch him, her head lifted from the pillow, her expression wary.

He sat then reached out sideways and patted her shoulder, feeling awkward. "You liked Abby's cats, right?"

She nodded.

He drew his hand back. "Did you ever hear the story of Puss in Boots?"

She shook her head.

"Do you want me to tell you the story? Puss is a cat, and he's the hero of the story."

She nodded.

He relaxed and only then realized how tense he'd been. "It was my grandfather's favorite fairy tale. He liked it because Puss was enterprising and proactive. Two of his favorite qualities." He peered at the girl. "Do you know what they mean?"

Her forehead crinkled. "It means they find out ways to do things."

"Exactly. You're very smart for a six-year-old." The thought slipped into his mind that his grandfather would have admired her. He would've admired Abby, too, from the moment she blackmailed him into getting her physics book. It would have brought on one of his rare bursts of laughter.

But he hadn't told his grandfather. They hadn't been on those terms.

He glanced at Cara. She was watching him, as if reserving judgment.

Though she wasn't his daughter by blood, she was a lot like him, after all.

He took a deep breath. "Once upon a time," he began, hearing his voice slow into a story mode instead of his normal curt and fast tone, "there was a miller with three sons and one cat...."

5

Day two, Abby thought. Though aware of Holden—too aware of him—she only gave him a brief glance, concentrating her attention on Cara as the two came into her house. Lion was at her side, his tail wagging happily, as she crouched and put her arms out.

Yesterday, Cara had looked at her nervously when she'd done this. Today she walked into her arms. Yesterday, she'd stood with her muscles stiff, as if uncertain what Abby would do. Today she leaned against her, but she trembled slightly.

Abby dropped a kiss on the top of her head, the same as she'd do for her cats or dog, before releasing her and straightening her legs.

"We're going to have a lovely day today." A *great* day, she thought. A day Cara would remember on days that were dark and lonely and she didn't know if she could stand it.

The way Abby remembered her mom and dad on the days when every step felt like she was walking through quicksand and would never make it through to the other side.

Cara looked at her with wide eyes then shifted her gaze to Lion, her arms reaching out.

Abby stepped out of the way as the girl embraced Lion with no hesitation. How wise of Cara to trust a dog more than a human.

Her heart squeezed.

Two weeks. Only two weeks.

That's what she'd thought yesterday. Eager for the two weeks to be over so she could go on with her life.

Watching Cara now, she changed her perspective. *Only nine days to show Cara a wonderful time. Four days left this week, five next week. Every day she was with her, there would be laughter. Every day kisses. Every day hugs.*

She looked up at Holden. His gaze was fixed on his daughter, his face unreadable.

Then he raised his eyes to her, and something in them, a bleakness, a need, made her suck in her breath. Made her want to step forward and hug him, too.

"I'll try to be here earlier tonight," he said.

"Try?" She reined in her volatile emotions. Maybe everyone needed a hug, but it didn't mean she had to do the hugging. "That's not a word I like. It's a wiggle word." She glanced down at Cara. "Like a wiggly worm."

Cara giggled, and Abby felt a thrill. A little catch of lightning flickering through her.

"What kind of worm would you prefer?" he asked.

She switched her gaze to him and felt his intensity. As if he really cared about her worm choices. "I've actually never met a worm I wanted to..." His eyes lit up, and she knew she should keep her mouth shut. But since the first time she'd seen him nine years ago and threatened to call the police on his brother, her shut-up valve hadn't seemed to work around him. A lot had changed in the past nine years, but not that. "Wiggle up to," she finished.

Cara giggled again then said, "Epic!" She knelt on the

floor and held her arms out to the white kitten. The normally timid kitten dashed straight to her, meowing and rubbing her head against her arms and her chin, marking her scent on Cara's skin.

A hand clasped Abby's shoulder, and she whipped her head up, staring at Holden who was staring at Cara. He didn't seem to be aware that he was standing so close that she felt his body heat. He didn't seem to be aware that he was holding onto her shoulder as if he had a right to touch her like this, as if she were more than just a babysitter.

She knew when his awareness returned, the intensity leaving his face, his muscles relaxing, his grasp loosening. She could feel his reluctance as he pulled his hand away slowly, his fingers brushing her shoulders in a caress that sent shivers through her.

"I'll be back by six," he said, his voice husky.

He told Cara goodbye. She looked up at him, her smile dipping. He headed to the door, and Abby followed him.

"So what are you going to be?" she asked. "A man or a worm?"

Gripping the screen-door handle, he turned slightly. His gaze flickered up and down her, and she was aware of her peach T-shirt with the cat outline and old, silky, blue shorts that she liked because cat and dog hair slid right off them, while her hair was barely combed and her face was clean of makeup. But none of that mattered because she could tell by the smoldering in his light blue eyes—no longer *icy* blue—that he saw her as a man saw a woman.

Some things a woman always knew.

"The first time I saw you," he said, "you know what I thought?"

"No."

"That you were trouble." He nodded then opened the door and headed outside. But even after the door closed behind him, she felt his stare on her face and body, as if it were burned into her skin. As if he'd branded her with his gaze just like Epic had branded Cara with her pheromones.

Abby wrapped her arms around herself, a frisson whispering through her.

Men. It was too bad she couldn't put them in a little box and just take them out when she needed them.

Which wouldn't be that often.

She mentally locked the box and imagined herself kicking it, the box going up, up, up in the sky, disappearing into the sun.

Only then did she turn back to Cara and to her pets. Her reality. And though it would be great to have no money worries, and a lot of women her age already had a husband, kids, and a 401K account, she felt full inside. In this moment, she was alive and happy, and she had a little girl to take to a dog park for the first time in her life.

And when they were finished with the park, then she would come home and worry about what came next.

————

Will that man be at the dog park? Quigley asked. *The one who came to the house the last time?*

Minnie hissed at Quigley's reminder of Mom's last

mistake. *If he comes, I'll scratch him again.*

Lion said if he sees that man, he'll bite him. A humming sound came from Quigley's throat, and he jumped up to the top of the cat-perch ladder. *I would like that. Mom should be more careful who she mates with. He was a bad man.*

Humans are like dogs, Minnie advised him. Epic was napping, and she thought it looked like a good idea. *They're too trusting.*

Is Cara's dad good? Quigley asked.

Minnie took a quick lick of her front paw. Next would be her back paw. *I don't know yet. Did you smell him?*

The air stank with his mating smell. Did you smell her, too?

How could I miss it? The mating scent is stronger than tuna.

What are we going to do?

She lay down, not answering. She didn't want to go through another of Abby's romances again. She'd rather go to the bad place, the one called "the vet," with the ladies who poked her with needles.

Maybe this time will be better, Quigley said. *Maybe he'll be good for her. And good for us, too. Maybe he'll help save us.*

She gave him a long look. He was younger but old enough to know better. *We'll do just fine without him, the way we've always done. Mom will save us, and if she doesn't...*

I know, Quigley said, *we'll have to do it ourselves.* And then he braced himself and hissed, the way he stood making Minnie think of a bird with its chest puffed out to attract the females, pretending to be big, strong, and wise.

Human males did the same thing. And human females did it, too, only in different ways.

The way Mom had this morning.

Minnie hunched down. She had to trust in Mom...but maybe there was a way they could help her make everything go right.

She would just have to watch out for the right opportunity.

When it came, she would pounce on it.

6

Holden entered Ryan's office, and Ryan's eyebrows rose with surprise. He was sitting back, a phone to his ear. He held up two fingers, which Holden took to mean he'd be off in two minutes.

Instead of sitting, Holden headed to the window and peered out at the view of the employee parking lot. Usually he drove in, parked in his reserved spot, and didn't give the rest of the lot another thought. But here he could glance out and see the two empty rows in the back that used to be filled.

In the view from his office, he could see the building that used to hum with workers and noise ten years ago. But he couldn't actually see the emptiness. He couldn't actually hear the silence in it.

It helped him ignore the problem. But today he couldn't ignore anything. He felt like the prince and the pea, and the pea was the size of a parking lot and damned uncomfortable, gnawing at his belly.

"What's up?" Ryan asked.

Holden turned. "I saw your text about the Houston account."

"They're downsizing. Judy has a couple new leads."

He headed to Ryan's desk. "If this keeps up, we'll have to downsize. So far, we haven't laid off or fired anyone. We've just not rehired when people retire or quit. It's not good. A company is either growing or dying. And we're dying."

"Hey, I've been saying that for years."

"Funny, I haven't heard you say anything."

Ryan's face reddened. "Maybe I haven't said it, but I've been thinking it. It's the reason I went to Miami instead of Italy last January. And I'm more careful with my investments. If the business goes under, I should be good."

Hot anger surged through Holden. "What about our workers?"

"Most of them are older." Ryan got up and stepped to the window then turned to face him.

Like two gunslingers standing off in a saloon, Holden thought.

"If we go under," Ryan continued, "they'll be okay."

"But what about the city?" Holden gestured toward the heart of the city. "Eagleton Furniture is a mainstay of the community. We still have 435 workers. They buy groceries here, go to schools, restaurants, clinics, the movies. They shop here. What we decide to do, even the smallest decisions, have a large ripple effect on Eagleton's economy."

Ryan shoved his hands in his pockets. "Anything we do, the Asian factories can copy and do cheaper a month later. We still have the high-end stores buying our stuff, but even there..." He shook his head. "I don't like it any more than you do."

Holden didn't reply right away, the silence stretching between them as a truck drove down the parking lot, its motor rumbling, and a hawk flew by Ryan's window.

"We need to stop being complacent," Holden said. "We need to stop letting ourselves off the hook."

Ryan took his hands out of his pockets. "That's easy for you to say. It's not as easy to do."

"Maybe it's not supposed to be easy. Maybe life isn't supposed to be easy. I don't think it was easy for our great-grandfather to start the business, either."

"What do you suggest?"

Holden shook his head. "We're stale. We need to do something."

Ryan braced his legs. "No matter what you think of me, our reps aren't slackers. We're aware that we're losing customers to cheaper foreign competitors. We're doing everything we can to find new markets."

The anger leaked out of Holden. "You can't fix it until I fix it. We've gotten stale. We need to revitalize the company. Shake things up."

Ryan's eyebrows rose again...then kept on rising. "What the hell did you do with my brother?" He grinned. "Funny, I thought having a child killed brain cells, but it's fired up yours."

"Something has," Holden said, and an image opened in his mind of Abby laughing. Since he'd seen her on Monday, his brain wasn't his only organ that had fired up.

This was the fourth day this week he'd seen her. When he'd dropped off Cara this morning, he'd tried to stop himself from looking forward to Abby's grin and the way she seemed to laugh at him and, at the same time, laugh with him. As if they shared a secret.

But besides Cara's parentage, his only secret was the way his body reacted around her.

Ryan headed to his desk, diverting his thoughts. "Are

you going to call a meeting?"

"Not yet." He spoke slowly. In his mind, he could feel...something. His hand tingled, the way it did sometimes when he was alone at night, or even in his office, and he needed to paint. "Let's both of us think about it."

He took long strides to the door. "Call if you have any ideas," he said and headed across the hall to his office. After letting Sherry know he didn't want to be interrupted, he brought out his paints. Normally he didn't do this here, but once in a while, the need became irresistible. The way he imagined a junkie needed a hit or Sherry, a self-proclaimed chocoholic, needed her top drawer filled with chocolate.

Methodically, he prepared for the painting. He cleared his desk and set down this morning's newspaper to protect his desk. He got out his paints and a canvas. He went into his private bathroom for water.

He did all this in a trancelike state, his conscious thoughts at a minimum. He finally sat down at his desk and stared at the blank canvas for a long moment.

Then his hand twitched, and he chose a cerulean blue. Squirted it on the plastic plate he used as a palette. Then he added some white. As he dipped in his brush, mixing the colors, he didn't know what he was going to paint....

He'd never told anyone, not Juliana, and certainly not Portia, but at times like this it felt as if his subconscious ruled his actions.

Taking a deep breath, he put brush to canvas, and his brush started to fly.

————

He set down his brush, looked at the image of a cat with red-gold hair and green eyes. The colorful cat sat on a purple velvet chair with wheels, like a cross between a fairy-tale carriage and a chair.

Like all his pictures, it appeared to be suspended in ether, giving it a fantastical appearance. This time, the background was pale blue, reminding him of the summer sky.

It was trying to tell him something. He connected the coloring of the cat to Abby but had no idea what it meant.

It wasn't a painting of her naked. That would have needed no interpretation.

Now he had *that* image in his brain, and he went to his bathroom to clean his brushes and put away his supplies and put the painting on top of a bookcase shelf to dry.

Only then did the problems of his business become paramount in his mind again. He called Sherry and told her he was taking off early, something he rarely did because it set a bad example for his workers. He had no pressing appointments, and he needed fresh air. Sometimes his best ideas came when he was away from the source of his problems. In his case, the business.

Instead, he'd be going straight into another problem: his attraction to Abby.

He stood, and his heart beat harder, and his blood flowed faster, and he felt more alive than he had for years. His whole life, he'd done the right thing, the responsible thing. Even marrying Juliana had seemed responsible on paper. Her family was wealthier than his; she knew the best people; she was beautiful, well-traveled, and healthy.

What he hadn't known was that she was like a beautiful rose on the verge of rotting. But now he knew a woman who laughed a lot, who sparkled like the sunlight on the lake and glowed like the moon, was not a woman who would stay with a man like him.

Twenty minutes later, he reached Abby's house, and her sister told him that Abby and Cara weren't there.

7

The music was loud, but Minnie still heard the buzzing of bees, the brush of wind outside, and the car engine coming down the driveway.

On a series of boxes halfway up to the high barn ceiling, she crouched, recognizing the low growl of the engine. The sound was smooth, though not as smooth—or as wonderful—as her purr.

The car stopped, and the music changed to another song with a faster beat. Craning her head toward the driveway, she filtered out the music and listened hard, catching the click of the car door opening. She sniffed deeply, and through the smells of trees, leaves, sky, sun, people, and wood, she scented *him*.

She became still. Abby had brought her here so she could try out the new furniture. Sam's cats were too wild and unreliable to test the furniture. And too messy. Quigley wasn't much better. If he smelled a squirrel or a rabbit, or even a bird, he might chase after it—and then get scared to be alone in the grass. So Mom had picked her to do it.

A wise choice, though if Minnie smelled a mouse, it would be her duty to go after it.

So far that hadn't happened.

The only animal she smelled that didn't belong here was a just a man.

She remained in the crouched position, all her senses aware, storing everything the humans said or did in her mind to share later with Quigley and Lion.

If she could trust the humans to do the right thing, she would happily nap in the sun instead of spying on them. But it was a fact that she was a smart cat. A *very* smart cat. Smarter than humans. Humans seemed to think because they were bigger they were wiser.

But if they were so smart, why was the world in such a mess?

Yet some of them were good people. Like Mom and Grace and Sam. And Holden was Cara's father and Daisy's nephew, so Minnie held out hope for him.

And then there was the way he smelled when he was around Mom.

And the way she smelled back.

Things were changing in their house. And they could change for the worse or they could change for the better. Anything that happened between Mom and Holden today might be important.

———

The double barn doors were open with music pouring out, some girl singing that hips don't lie, and Holden had to agree with the singer. There was a black pickup truck and a red SUV in the driveway. He glanced in the SUV and saw the child's car seat in the back. A small knot of tension inside him unknotted.

Of course Abby had a child's seat. When Abby's sister had told him she'd taken Cara to "the barn," he'd worried. He should have known better. He'd already concluded she wouldn't do anything that would hurt Cara.

He was the first to admit that he didn't trust easily; no one with his background would trust easily.

The barn doors were opened, and he entered the brightly lit place that he supposed had once held hay or other products. Maybe animals or tractors and other farm machines. Right now it was filled with odd-sized and -shaped furniture. To his right, he saw Abby talking to a woman who towered over her. Then his eyes were drawn to Cara, sitting on one of the cat perches, her little face bright with laughter.

He stopped. Emotion filled him, clogging his throat, a reaction to her happy face. It didn't matter if she was his or not; every child deserved to be happy.

The thought crept into his mind that soon—in just nine days—she would be taken away from this. She would be sent back to the loveless place where she was treated as a duty. A place that wasn't a home but a void that would suck the happiness right out of her soul.

"Holden?" Abby called, her voice raised to be heard above the music.

He turned to her, but overcome by the unjustness, he couldn't speak for a moment. He knew a little of what Cara was going through. When he was her age, at least he'd had his brother with him. Though it wasn't the same as having loving parents, it was something.

The tall woman held up a remote, her thumb moved, and the music shut off.

"What are you doing here?" Abby asked.

"I took off work early and stopped by your house. Your sister said you were here."

"You wanted to see Cara?" She gave him a radiant

smile then turned to Cara. "Did you hear that, Cara? Your daddy came here to see you."

He shifted his gaze to Cara. Her smile was gone, her face solemn, her eyes searching his face, as if checking to see if what Abby said was true.

There was no way he could tell them he didn't know why he'd come here. That he—who always did something with a purpose—had just...driven here.

But maybe his coming here had been with a purpose. A purpose driven by his unconscious mind.

Because of the painting.

Because, at the most basic level, he wanted to see Abby.

"Do you want to tell me about this place?" he asked Cara.

She blinked and turned to Abby.

"Tell your daddy." Abby smiled her encouragement.

Her words started a constriction in his chest, as if his heart had squeezed into the shape of a clay ball. He remembered all the times his parents would breeze into his grandparents' house, staying just long enough to get more money before they left. Hardly paying any attention to him or Ryan.

It was true that people married their parents—that's what he'd done with Juliana.

Not the second time around. When he and Portia decided to have children, he had no doubts that she would read all the books, buy the right foods and products, do the correct things. She would do everything by the book, as would he. They wouldn't be spontaneous joy givers like Abby, but they would be responsible parents.

Cara started to push off the perch, and he took quick steps forward to be there in case she slid onto the hard ground. She landed with a stumble then caught herself.

"Good girl," he said.

Though her lips didn't curve into a smile, she held her hand out to him. He took it, and the constriction in his chest melted, and it felt like his closed clay ball of a heart opened a crack.

"This is cat furniture." She made a sweeping gesture that encompassed the many pieces, her wide eyes showing her amazement of this place of wonders.

Glancing around, he gave the feline furniture his attention. There were at least a couple dozen designs. Against the wall was something that looked like a puzzle of boxes, each one a different color. It looked fun, and he suspected Abby had designed it.

"Look up there," Cara said, pointing at the high barn ceiling.

He gazed up. Attached to ropes from the rafters, a series of boxes were suspended about four feet above his head. Some sort of a walkway for cats. A familiar face with Siamese blue eyes peered down at him. *Minnie.* As if she was spying on him.

Shaking his head, he turned his gaze to the furniture in front of him. The cat probably belonged to Abby's partner, because who would use a cat as a spy?

"Amazing." He peered more closely at a lopsided, ladder-like design with perches that was similar to the one in his aunt's condo. This one was in cherry, one of the most durable woods used for furniture. One of his favorites, and it wasn't a cheap wood, either.

"Custom?" he asked.

Abby nodded. "For a friend of your aunt's."

"Great work. Very smooth."

"Thank you," the taller woman said, her voice brisk.

Holden turned to her. She was only a couple inches shorter than him, tall and shapely, with pleasant features, though her short haircut didn't flatter her long face. Holden held out his hand. Her grip was firm, and he felt calluses on the pads of her fingers.

"You must be Sam," he said. "My fiancée, Portia Engell, has good things to say about you."

Her eyebrows rose. "That's Portia. Always good."

"Don't you like good?"

Her head tilted, and he had the feeling she was inwardly laughing. "There's a reason I work out here while Abby chats up the clients."

"That's me." Abby grinned at Cara. "The chatty one."

Cara giggled.

"How are the conditions here for working?" he asked Sam.

"I manage."

"*We* manage," Abby said, drawing his attention.

"I thought you worked in your home." He looked at her, and it felt as if her smile meant something special for him. Then he told himself she was one of those people who made everyone feel they were special, like the best salesmen did—and the best whores and the best politicians. But even that knowledge didn't stop him from feeling better about himself, better about life, just from the approving look in her eyes.

"I help design," she said. "And I cut out the carpets for the perches."

"She does." Sam's smile was indulgent, as if Abby were her little sister. "I measure and tell her what's possible and what's not. Otherwise, she'd promise the world."

"Everyone deserves the world." Abby bent toward Cara. "You deserve the world. Isn't that right?"

Cara didn't answer, and Holden saw the pucker on her forehead and the way she bit her lip. And in her eyes, he saw something else. A *want* for something she couldn't have.

He knew that want. He'd had it when he was young and saw happy families laughing and talking together, teasing each other.

It wasn't good to have a want like that.

"I think Cara knows what she wants," he said, "and it's not the world."

"What do you want?" Abby asked her.

"Epic." She stared at Abby, but the small tips of her fingers curled tightly around his first three fingers. "I want Epic to be mine."

Abby's eyes shot up, her gaze meeting his and staying. There was silence as another song came on, a woman singing about the glory of love. And he felt as if someone kicked him in the chest.

And then he dragged his gaze from Abby's, because something odd was going on here. Something too deep, and maybe it was Cara, and maybe it was Abby, and maybe it was the uncertainty about his business, but he looked at Cara and said, "Yes."

Her mouth opened, and he could see she didn't believe him. Didn't believe he was telling the truth. Didn't believe that all the years of hearing "no" had changed in one second. That he would make this one dream come true.

"Yes, you can keep the kitten," he said, enunciating clearly so she could hear him over the song.

"Will *they* let me keep it?" Cara asked, her voice so soft he had to bend forward to hear her.

Anger flashed through him; no need to ask who *they* were. And only after she pulled her hand from his and backed away from him did he realize his facial muscles were rigid and his eyes burning.

He relaxed his muscles, but her expression remained wary. "I'm not mad at you," he said. He could have gone on a tirade about her mother and grandparents, but it would scare her, and she'd be afraid to say anything to him, afraid to get that reaction again. He knew that because he'd lived that. "I'm mad at...someone else. Don't worry. I'll make sure your grandmother and grandfather let you keep Epic. They owe you that."

Again he felt her stare, then a tentative smile pushed up the corners of her lips, and then it widened and opened to a big one. Her eyes glowed brightly, and he was still bending forward to hear what she would say when her arms whipped up, her small hands curving around his neck, not quite reaching together at the nape of it, and she leaned the top of her head against his chest.

His instinct was to jerk away, but he froze instead. After a second, he reached down to clumsily pat her back, aware of the silence in the big barn, hearing only the slam of his own heartbeat.

"I love you, Daddy." Cara pulled back.

He had no choice but to say the words. If he didn't say them back, she would be devastated. And he was acutely aware of Abby and Sam watching and listening. But none of that mattered, because there was a strange *feeling* in his heart, as if there were a clamp about it, squeezing and squeezing until it was ready to burst.

He couldn't remember how long it had been since he'd felt like this. Or, indeed, if he'd ever felt like this.

"I love you, too." He heard the roughness of his voice, and he felt something wet on his cheeks. He wondered what it was. Something leaking from the barn roof, which wouldn't be good for the furniture.

Her hands came up, and she touched his face, wiping across his cheekbone with the tip of her finger. "You're crying," she said, wonder in her voice.

"I never cry," he said.

She just stared at him, and then she smiled and patted her hand on his cheek, the same way he imagined she would pet the dog.

He straightened, and only then did he turn his head to the women. No, *woman*, he thought, his gaze resting on Abby's eyes. Seeing their softness and approval, both of which felt pretty good to him.

Too good.

Something strange was happening to him, and he had to leave now. He felt as if he'd fallen down into Wonderland, where things weren't like anything in the real world. Not even his heart that seemed to be melting.

"I have to leave." He gazed down at Cara. "I have to go

back to work. I'll pick you up at six, right?"

"Me and Epic," she said.

He stiffened but nodded. He'd given her his word. "Yes, you and Epic."

She smiled at him again, a shy smile. He patted the top of her head, feeling awkward. Both of them were learning how to do this family thing, though she wasn't his family and would be taken away in a week and two days.

"I'll see you later." He backed away from her. Nodding at the two women, he saw the glistening eyes of Abby. While Sam's were narrowed in cynicism, as if she didn't believe his show of affection.

He strode away and wished he didn't believe in it, either. He didn't know what had happened, or how, but he needed to get out before he did anything else imprudent and unlike him.

8

"He's engaged," Sam said.

Abby straightened her shoulders, wondering what Sam saw in her face. "I know. Don't worry about me. He's not my type. Too serious. *Life* is serious, and when I go out, I like to laugh and have fun. He's like a..." She gestured outdoors. "A sturdy oak tree that just stands there and provides shade and oaks. I *like* oak trees. I admire them. But in the end, he's a tree, and I prefer a flower."

"I've seen a few of your laughing boyfriends." Sam scratched the side of her head, riffling her short hair. "They remind me of dandelions."

Abby laughed, and Cara giggled.

"Do you like dandelions?" Sam bent toward Cara.

Cara nodded energetically. "They're pretty."

"Right," Sam said, "pretty and bright-colored, but then you wake up one morning, and they're dandelion fluff, blowing away with the wind."

Abby made a face. So true about her boyfriends through the years. "But what if I don't mind them blowing away?"

Sam shook her head, one side of her mouth indenting. "Nothing wrong with a girl having fun."

"But I'm not a girl anymore. Right?" Abby winced at the truth of her words. Though she still got carded, thirty was coming up in less than two years, and she was still living from month to month. And with the extra expenses—the leaking roof and the machinery breaking—this month it was week to week.

"When I get my life together," Sam said, "that's when I'll give you advice."

"Ha! So true." Abby shook off this pensive mood. She didn't do pensiveness well. It usually ended with her diving into a depression that even a bag of her favorite chocolate couldn't make disappear, until she recovered enough to remind herself she had so much good that meant more than money. She had her health, her sister, her cats, her dog, her friends. And though her parents were gone now, she'd had wonderful years with them.

All she was missing was money.

"I don't have time for a serious relationship anyway," she said.

"Just the fun ones?" Sam asked. "How's that working for you?"

"Bitch."

Cara gasped, and Sam leaned forward, her hands on her thighs, and looked Cara in the eyes. "Cara, I'm proud of being a bitch. It's what people call you when you tell the truth." She straightened and peered straight into Abby's eyes. "But I know something about love; it's the serious ones that stick."

"But what if I like to laugh?"

"Don't tell me. Tell it to your heart."

"You're..." Words wouldn't come. At least none she could say in front of Cara.

"Right. I'm right." Sam folded her arms.

"He's engaged. I'm not likely to get into any trouble with him."

"I know Portia. She and he would make a terrible couple. They're too alike. I bet their sex life is so boring they fall asleep in the middle—"

"Sam!" Abby put her hand on Cara's shoulder.

Scratching the back of her neck, Sam shook her head. "Good thing I don't have children. I'd be a terrible mom."

"You'd be wonderful!"

"I wish you were my mom," Cara said, her voice wobbly.

In an instant, Abby snapped around and knelt at Cara's feet, hugging her close against her. She wanted to tell her that she wished Cara were *her* daughter. But saying that would be irresponsible and might even hurt the girl.

Two thin arms curled around Abby's neck, hugging her back, and Cara's forehead pressed against her neck. Seconds later, Abby felt moisture on her neck. Still on her knees, smelling cut wood and wood stain and small girl, Abby swayed, rocking Cara from side to side, crooning wordlessly and wishing she had a secret power to make everything all right for her.

And thinking that if she were married to Holden— which was crazy thinking—she and he could petition for custody.

She loosened her grip. Time for her real life, which didn't involve a multimillionaire who would make Prince Charming look too pretty. Like the furniture his company made, he exuded solidity.

Cara let go of her. "Are we going to be here much longer?"

Abby stood then wiped wood dust from her knees.

"You want to go home to Epic?" Cara's vigorous nods made Abby smile.

Her underarms and her breasts prickled from the heat. It was in the lower eighties today and humid. She glanced at Sam. "We should put the fans on."

"Can we afford it?" Sam asked.

"Can we afford not to?"

"The electric bills are in my name. If I can't pay it, my credit will be mud."

Abby looked around at the big barn they couldn't heat adequately in winter or cool in summer.

If only they could charge more.

If only they could afford more.

If only they had more money.

"We'll have the money soon. I've decided to sell the house." She forced her voice to be steady, forced her shoulders not to droop.

She'd been fooling herself that two weeks would make a difference. The queen of positive thinking was finally admitting that wishing it were so didn't make it so.

Sam's eyebrows rose. "Where will you sleep?"

"We'll be all right."

"Don't say your SUV."

"It's a big SUV." Abby laughed and heard the shakiness in her voice. "Just kidding. Once I sell the house, I'll have money to afford an apartment for me and Grace." Swallowing, she pictured the big house in the exclusive area where she and Grace had started out. She'd traded that in for the smaller house soon after they realized there was no money. That the unlicensed, drunk driver who'd smashed his van into their parents' car hadn't had insurance. And that her parents had been brilliant in their professions but not brilliant at making sure their daughters would be cared for financially.

Abby had never faulted them for it. They hadn't planned to die so soon.

"You could stay here," Sam said, her voice gruff, but Abby shook her head. They'd gone through this before.

"It's not fair to Grace to give up her friends."

"It's not fair to you to give up your life."

She shrugged. "I haven't given my life away. I'm living every second." She smiled at her friend. "We'll manage."

"You could use the money to pay a factory in China to make the cat furniture." Sam's eyes wouldn't meet Abby's. "I'll be okay doing something else."

"No." Abby spoke firmly. "We're in this together. I believe in what we're doing. We're putting out a quality product, and the people who purchase our furniture love it. We just need time, and I'm not giving up."

Sam's tight shoulders sloped in relief. Only then did Abby realize she'd been worried about her answer. Abby didn't know Sam's whole story but was familiar enough to know that behind her stoic front was a woman who'd been deeply hurt.

Maybe because of Sam's sexuality, but she wasn't saying, and Abby wasn't asking. She loved Sam as a friend and admired her for her work ethic and her skills, and wasn't that what mattered?

Life wasn't about money. It was about love.

She said she had to get going and turned to call Minnie to her carrier. A meow caught her attention, Minnie at her feet already. She gazed down at her. "You must be the smartest cat in the world."

Sam patted Cara's head then looked at Abby with a twisted smile.

"I think it's way past time that I should call my old sorority sister."

"Are you going to ask her to help us?" Abby should be glad that Sam was trying to raise money.... But the thought that it was Holden's fiancée made her feel sick.

"No." Sam smiled with her lips together, but her eyes...they were narrowed, with no smile in them at all.

Abby nodded and turned away. As she and Cara walked out of the barn, the sun hit them, bright and hot, but it felt good on her shoulders and face. A small hand slipped into hers. They stopped at the car, and a tug on her hand made Abby turn around.

"What I said about Sam being my mom?" Cara blinked, her little face twisted with worry. "I was being nice. I wish *you* were my mom."

Abby knelt once again and hugged her. Maybe Cara was collecting hugs, committing them to memory for when she had to go back to that loveless place she'd come from.

A few moments ago, Abby had thought silence was the responsible thing to do.

But now she thought she'd been wrong.

"Me, too," she whispered. "Me, too."

9

In his office, Holden stared at the canvas for long moments until his cell phone rang, three smooth beats. Portia's ring. He put the canvas in his briefcase then grabbed the phone. Forcing his facial muscles and his jaw to relax, he greeted her.

"Do you mind if I cancel dinner tonight?" she asked.

He tilted back in his chair. "That's fine. Something else come up?"

"Remember we talked about my old sorority sister? Sam?"

"I met her today."

"Did you?" Her tone changed, and he imagined her frowning, thinking about their meeting and wondering what it meant.

"I went to the barn and saw their cat furniture."

"Oh, that's right. Abby's your babysitter. I was so excited to hear from Sam again that I forgot about it. She just...disappeared from my life. We were such good friends, too. I never knew why, and it's bothered me all these years. She wants to meet for dinner tonight, and I said yes. I didn't think you'd mind."

"I'm glad that she called you. You go ahead and enjoy yourself."

She laughed and sounded giddy, unlike herself. "I plan to. You have a nice dinner with Cara."

A knock came on his door, then Ryan strode in, as usual not waiting for an invite. Holden sat straight and said goodbye to Portia and hung up, glad that he'd put the painting away and Ryan wouldn't see it.

"What was that?" Ryan sat on the leather guest chair, one foot slung over his knee. "You got a big order? You're looking..." His eyes narrowed. "Relieved."

"That was Portia. She called to cancel dinner for tonight."

Ryan laughed, though nothing about this situation was funny to Holden. He couldn't deny his relief, but he didn't like feeling it.

"Dude, you sure don't look like a man in love. You should cancel the wedding."

"Love fades. Compatibility is the key to a good marriage."

"Bullshit."

"Since when did you become the expert on relationships? I didn't ask Portia to marry me on a whim. I put a lot of thought into it."

"That's the problem. It's not thought that you need to put into it."

"What?" Holden raised one eyebrow. "The heart?"

"Nah." Ryan grinned. "The penis."

"In that case, you should be asking strippers at the VaVaVoom Bar to marry you."

His brows rose. "Ha, ha, ha. Don't turn this around to me. I'm not the one about to make the second biggest mistake in my life."

"Right. You're the one not making any mistakes. When was your last serious relationship? What's the matter? Why are you afraid to commit?"

"Told you, it's not me." Ryan gave him the same smile

that made women slip him their phone numbers and bra sizes. "It's my penis."

"Your penis drives your brains. Now I know your problem."

"Every man thinks with his penis when it comes to women." He nodded his chin at Holden. "Except you. And that's your big problem. Your marriage to Portia will be like Grandma and Grandpa's."

"They were married for sixty years before Grandma died."

"And I'm sure they were sixty looooong years. How often do you think they had sex?"

Holden shuddered. "I don't even want to think about that."

"Neither did they. There was a reason our father was an only child."

"You're an asshole."

Ryan shrugged. "I'm telling it as I see it. When was the last time you and Portia got sweaty together?"

Holden glared at him, his lips clamped together.

If he said anything out loud, Ryan would know.

Ryan unhooked his leg from his knee and sat up straight. "Shit, don't tell me. You aren't having sex with her."

Holden stood, wishing he'd never come back this afternoon. "What Portia and I do or don't do isn't any of your damn business." He grabbed his suit jacket. "I've had it for the day. I'm going home early. If any important calls come in, I'll tell Sherry you can take them."

"Yeah, but can you trust me?" Ryan grinned again, but his shoulders were stiff, and his gaze didn't leave

Holden's face.

"If I didn't trust you, you think I'd let you take care of the business?"

A ripple of emotion flashed through Ryan's face, then he looked the same, still grinning, but the tension gone. And as Holden stepped past him, Ryan grabbed his arm, and now his grin was gone, too, the serious look on his face making him appear more mature and less of an overgrown frat boy.

"Hey, I don't give a damn who sleeps with who—except my own sleeping partners. I'm concerned that you're making another huge mistake. The first time out, you married a woman just like Mom, and that was disaster number one. This time you're marrying Grandma. I can practically see disaster number two coming."

Holden stared at his brother. "If you need to know, we did have sex."

His brother's forehead creased. "You 'had sex.' Like, it was once?"

"I'm not talking about this anymore." He jerked his arm away, grabbed his briefcase, and strode out. He was leaving early, but this day was a bust. And no way was he going to tell his brother that the sex was fine. That it happened the night he'd proposed to her, and she'd said yes.

She'd been a virgin, the fact shocking him. Pleasing him. Not because he wanted to be a woman's only lover. It pleased him because it was proof of her self-control and that, after their wedding, she wouldn't turn into a wild child like Juliana.

So what if fireworks hadn't gone off? After all, she wasn't experienced. And after that one time, she'd asked if he minded if they waited until after the wedding "to do it again."

Even if their lovemaking didn't get better with marriage, it wouldn't matter. It wasn't as if most married couples he knew had a hot sex life. Years of living together had a way of making sex dull. But if you had respect and shared values, it could still be a good marriage.

His brother was a fool. That's what marriage was about.

But as he walked away, his mind wanted to stop thinking about Portia and think instead about Abby. About the way she loved so much. If Juliana was like his mother and Portia his grandmother, Abby was like no one else he knew.

She was the unknown.

And like most men, he felt the urge to explore the unknown.

But he wasn't most men, and he could and would control himself.

He was raised to resist temptation, and a small, sexy redhead wasn't going to break him.

10

"We didn't expect you so early," Abby said, standing in the kitchen, knowing her face was turning an unlovely shade of pink that clashed with her hair. She reminded herself that Holden was engaged, and it didn't matter if her face turned green or purple. He was off-limits. "You may as well stay for dinner."

He stared at her for a long moment, and she stared back. She felt his awareness of her, warmth prickling through her skin.

"This is awkward," she said. From her sister's bedroom came the voices of Cara and Grace, both excited and happy as Grace went through her jewelry box, giving Cara old jewelry that was too childish for her.

"My coming early?"

"No, this thing between us." She was glad the girls were in the other room. It was good to say this. Good to get it out in the open.

He stood still, his eyes never leaving hers. She kept her chin up.

"I'm glad I'll only have to see you for six more days," she said.

His eyes gleamed, and she was reminded that men were hunters and went after what they couldn't have.

Too bad. He was engaged, and that was that. Engaged men had their hunting licenses revoked. There were always the ones who hunted illegally, but from the little she knew of Holden, he was the kind of man who did everything legally and with honor.

Besides, she knew his fiancée—vaguely, and it had been a long time ago. Just an hour ago, she'd looked up Portia's images online. There were quite a few photos of her at different events, and it was not fun for Abby, who had been hoping she'd put on a few pounds or that her complexion wasn't as flawless anymore.

None of that had happened. Portia looked like a model. Tall and slender with a pale complexion and dark hair in a pixie cut.

Abby couldn't imagine herself in a pixie cut. Her hair would look like red fuzz, and her eyes would be too big. The only time she would ever want that look would be on Halloween. And even then, she would scare small children coming to her door. They'd run to their parents screaming, and she'd stand on the porch feeling awful, stuck with a bagful of candy.

"So you have a thing for me," he said.

"And you have a thing for me," she said.

He stared at her. "I'm engaged."

"I hope you keep remembering that."

"I don't forget."

"You should call Portia and see her tonight. Cara can sleep over with us." With each word, she was punishing herself, but she needed this punishment. Needed it to stop these emotions that she had no business feeling. "You're not my type, anyway. I usually go for guys who are more fun."

"And you're not mine. I usually date women who are more... Just more."

"Is that a cut on my height?" Now her voice rose with

indignation, when she wanted to be aloof and uncaring.

He was holding back laughter; she could see it in the clenched muscles around his mouth and the small lines raying out from the corners of his eyes. Usually she loved laughter, even when the joke was on her. Maybe even more in that case. But now... Well, sometimes a girl just didn't feel like laughing. Once again, she had to fight to keep from kicking him in the shins.

Or higher.

"No insult intended," he said.

"Because I am more." She held her arms out at her sides. "I am so filled with life that when I was young, I would climb up on the roof and yell that I could fly."

He laughed, a rumble that came from his belly, joy in his face. "I can picture you doing that. What happened to that little girl?"

She tilted her head. "Are you kidding? I still think I could fly."

"Aren't you missing something?"

"A pair of wings. That's all I need."

"I was going to say an airplane ticket."

"That's the difference between us."

"The difference between us,"—he leaned toward her and lowered his face, until their lips were a hand-width away—"is that I already picture you with wings."

As she gasped, a voice called out, "Daddy!"

He jerked back, looking guilty.

So he should feel guilty, Abby thought fiercely. He was flirting with her. Trying to seduce her.

And she was flirting back. Trying to seduce him.

That was the last time she started a conversation with

a man by telling him to stay away. Obviously it was a case of wanting what they shouldn't take and what she couldn't give.

But his attention was on Cara now, as she padded into the kitchen, her eyes shining, but still too shy and insecure to run to him.

He held out his hand to her, his face different. Serious. As if he knew how fragile she was.

Coming up behind Cara, Grace frowned, her gaze flickering from Abby to him and back. Abby shifted her eyes away from Grace's. Her sister was old enough to feel the thickness in the atmosphere that happened when two people were shooting off their pheromones, creating a kind of sex soup.

"Good thing I made extra food tonight." Abby made her voice cheery, but it came out too loud and too forced. "Cara, your dad is joining us for dinner. You know where the plates and silverware are. Do you want to set a place at the table?"

Cara's flushed, happy face looked much better on a six-year-old than a twenty-eight-year-old, though Abby thought a happy face looked good on everyone. The world's best beauty secret.

Grace helped Cara set the table, and Abby served the food. The meal was simple: salad and spaghetti. There was plenty for everyone to eat. The conversation was lively with the girls talking about the cats and the dog. Though Cara didn't talk as much as her and Grace, she kept saying "my kitty," her face lit with happiness. Abby thought it was almost as if another little girl had taken over her body.

She glanced at Holden. He was frowning, and sudden anger flared inside her. She gripped the paper napkin on her lap, squishing it.

How could he have let this happen to his daughter? He seemed so solid, so trustworthy. How could he have neglected Cara like this?

In that second, he didn't look sexy to her anymore. With these thoughts inside her head, he wasn't even a man she liked.

His gaze switched to her, and she glared into his eyes, giving him the silent message that he'd lost her respect.

Yet she didn't look away. She wanted to ask him *Why? How? When?* As if there was a good reason for his neglect. The questions too many women asked of men when they did something wrong. Ready to grasp any excuse and say, "Yes, yes, yes, I see."

But the only good reason for neglect of a child was if you were seriously injured or if you didn't know about the child.

Or if you were dead.

He was none of those things.

She turned her head away and found it was easy to look away. Not all women would accept lame excuses. Not her.

Anyway, he was engaged, and it was nothing to do with her.

In a little over a week, Cara would be gone. After that, she would have no reason to see him again.

She would count down the days.

A small hand touched her arm, and she looked to her side at Cara, who gazed up at her with concern, as if she saw her unhappiness and was offering comfort.

Abby smiled and bent forward, putting her hand on the side of Cara's face. Cara leaned into her palm, much like Lion would do. And Abby felt her heart thump hard and steady as if new love poured into it, filling it. Love for this small girl who knew more than she should have about unhappiness.

An urge came over her to tell Cara that she wished she was her daughter, but she clamped her teeth together, holding back the words.

Yet tears burned her eyes as she pushed away her plate with spaghetti still on it. Cara took the hint and leaned away from her hand.

Good. She was too involved with this man and his daughter. She rescued dogs and cats, not an unhappily engaged man—because if he was happy, she was the wealthiest woman in the world—and his lost daughter.

"Anyone ready for ice cream?" she asked. And right then, she knew what she needed to do. It had started with Holden's Aunt Daisy. Who better to end it?

11

The house seemed empty once Cara, Epic, and Holden left. The dishwasher was on, and Grace was in her room. Abby settled in the living room, Minnie on her favorite perch next to her, Lion on the floor. Quigley wasn't around, and Abby guessed he was in Grace's room. Or the basement. Or one hundred other places to hide in.

Cats weren't like dogs. Cats went where cats wanted to go. In a closet. A drawer. Sleeping on her bed or, as had happened more times than she liked to recall, throwing up on her bed.

When it happened, she sighed and dealt with it. Just as she was dealing with her inappropriate feelings for Cara's dad.

She picked up the phone and called Daisy. As it rang, she petted Minnie, who was staring at her intently, as if she were remembering everything to convey to the others. The thought made Cara smile as Daisy answered the phone in her strong voice and asked how the babysitting was going.

"Wonderful." She pulled her hand from Minnie. "Grace and I and the animals love Cara. She took home a foster kitten. The agency already okayed it."

"That was fast. It took me longer to get approval."

"You aren't the CEO of one of the biggest companies in the city."

Daisy's full-throated laugh came through. Abby

waited for her to stop; she lived by the rule to never interrupt a laugh. "They trusted my recommendation, too," she added, "and I did say he's your nephew. But that's not why I called. Do you remember telling me that you'd found the perfect man to fix me up with?"

"Darling, that was months ago. He's not on the market anymore."

Abby wrinkled her nose. "Just as well, I suppose. Men are like vegetables. Leave them hang around too long and they get spoiled."

Daisy laughed again. "It's too bad. You would've been good for him."

"I don't want a man I can be good for. I want one who will be good for *me*."

"You're good for my soul," Daisy said, laughter still quivering in her full voice. "That's why I love you."

"If only you were a man, you'd be my perfect partner."

That set Daisy off again. Abby sat back in her chair and saw Minnie staring at her with her Siamese blue eyes.

"I do know an *im*perfect man," Daisy said, laughter still in her voice.

"Sounds good to me. Perfect is too much to live up to."

"What are you doing tonight?"

"Tonight?" Abby sat up straight. "I'm talking to you and will undoubtedly pet my cat. I might even go wild and pluck my eyebrows."

"Start plucking now. I'll call you back in five minutes."

Abby set down her phone and stared at Minnie.

"Wow. Daisy doesn't waste time."

Then she stood and headed to the bathroom. She needed to find her tweezers.

———————

Holden felt antsy tonight in his living room, his house too quiet. It was still light out, and he gazed out the French doors at the lake. Too many thoughts swirled in his head for him to sit and relax. Usually he worked late and went to bed early. Maybe reading a book in between or watching a favorite TV show or, when the urge hit him, painting one of his fantastical visions. Sometimes he and Portia would do something with friends, chatting and smiling, not saying anything of meaning that he could recall. Now he wondered what was behind their smiles. Happiness or loneliness or secret desires, hopes, and dreams.

He didn't know. He didn't even know Portia's hopes and dreams. Did she have any? She seemed to glide through life, doing everything exquisitely. She knew about his worries about the company. He'd told her the truth about Cara's parentage. Other than her, he'd only told Daisy and Ryan. It was their right to know the truth.

It wasn't Abby's right. But he'd seen the accusation and disappointment on her face at dinner tonight.

He'd seen the rejection. Yet he'd continued to eat his spaghetti as if nothing was wrong...when everything was wrong.

He'd burned at the injustice, yet he had no idea how to fix it.

A sound caught his attention. A soft meow.

Turning, he spotted the kitten.

"What are you doing here?" He bent and held his hand out for her to sniff.

The little ball of fluff did better than that. She rubbed the sides of her mouth on the bony ridges of his hand then tried to climb on it.

His mood softened. Epic stumbled off his hand, too big to fit. Still thinking she was tiny and obviously not accustomed to her growth spurts.

"I understand." He picked her up with both hands and held her in front of his face. "I think I'm more limber than I am, too."

Epic meowed.

"You're going to get white cat hair all over my brown couch, aren't you?"

Another meow.

"The lady at the pet store said I need to clean the litter box every day."

Another meow. As if she was answering him.

"The cleaning crew comes in only once a week. This means I'll have to do it myself."

The kitten didn't meow at him now, perhaps understanding that some subjects were better left unanswered.

"You're a smart kitten, aren't you?"

Epic meowed loudly, ending on a high note, as if it were an exclamation point.

"I agree. Let me give you a problem." Holden stepped to the brown, leather recliner and sank into it. "If I knew something that would change the way someone thought about me, do you think I should tell her?"

This time she mewled, a sound that could only be more positive if she'd nodded her small head.

"Even if it's not my secret?"

The kitten's head tilted, and she stared at him, as if trying to understand the subtext.

"Even if it would hurt another person if she found out the truth?" He frowned. Maybe it wouldn't have hurt Cara before this, he thought. But in these last couple days, she'd come to depend upon him. She'd told him she loved him.

Epic voiced a string of meows. Holden leaned back on the recliner and let her walk on his upper chest.

"That's definitely a yes," he said.

The kitten jumped off him, and he turned his head and watched her pad back down the hall toward Cara's bedroom.

He clasped the chair arms. If he thought Abby would say anything to Cara, he wouldn't talk to her. But of course she wouldn't. He got off his chair and went to the table where he'd left his cell phone. There was no excuse not to tell Abby.

A moment later, he listened to Grace tell him that Abby was on a date.

———

Mom and the man had driven away, but the man's smell lingered in the living room. The scent was familiar, and so was the man. Minnie remembered him from all the years ago, when she'd been very young. The man had petted her and had made Mom laugh.

Then he'd made Mom angry. And when Mom got

angry, so did Minnie.

She's with the wrong man, she told Quigley, who sat on the cat ladder's top perch. He liked being on top, and for the most part, Minnie let him go up there.

But every once in a while, she would run up and knock him down to the floor.

Just to show him who was really the boss.

She likes men who are wrong, Quigley said.

No, she doesn't. She says they're fun while they last.

What does that mean?

Minnie quickly licked a paw before replying. *It's like chasing a bug. It's fun for a while, but when you catch it, it's not as fun.*

It's fun for me. I eat bugs. If this man is wrong, I can scratch and bite him.

Let's wait. I didn't smell her mating scent before they left, just his.

Maybe this is about the business. Maybe that's why she left with him.

Minnie leaped up the ladder until she was on the perch below Quigley's. *Quigley, that's very smart of you.*

I can be smart.

Of course you can. Minnie reached up a paw and patted his head. It was important to encourage him when he did something right. Maybe he might even do it more often.

Then she turned and jumped down, perch by perch.

She would wait until Mom came home again. Then she would see if she should tell Quigley to use his claws to rip the man's face open.

———

Music spilled out of the bar, onto the sidewalk where Abby sat at a small table, holding a beer and leaning toward her surprise date. It was dusk out, day blending into night, and three young women walked past them, three young men following close behind, like bloodhounds after rabbits. Abby felt free and young herself tonight, her blood pulsing in time with the music.

"I still can't believe your aunt fixed me up with you." She grinned at Ryan Ramsay. He was still a hunk with his tousled, golden-blond hair and his bright blue eyes. He even came with dimples, the whole package. Maybe too much of a package. For her, at least. Already tonight, a couple young women had strutted by, giving him the eye and sticking out their assets, top and bottom, for him to ogle.

"You know what Aunt Daisy said?" he asked.

"That I was funny and cute and smart?"

He laughed. "That you were all wrong for me. We're too alike, and we wouldn't have a speck of attraction."

"And she's right." Abby lifted the beer to her mouth.

"Nope, she's wrong."

Abby fought to swallow the beer before she laughed. "You mean you'd do me?"

"In a second."

"A second? Is that how long you last?"

The waiter, stopping at their table with a cheeseburger and chips for him and fries for her, laughed.

Ryan grinned. When the waiter left, he said, "Hey, give me credit. I can go for at least twenty seconds."

She smiled at him, relaxed and in her zone. No tension, which was good. No sexual tension, which wasn't good.

In another time and place—the awful years after her parents had died—on the few nights Grace slept over at a friend's, she would've done him, too. Just to feel alive and wanted and not alone.

It was a good thing she hadn't run into him during those years. Not while...

Well, it didn't matter, she reminded himself. His brother was engaged to the perfect Portia, and she doubted they were celibate.

"Hey, something wrong with the fries?"

She shook her head and forced a smile. "They're greasy and unhealthy as hell. The best kind."

He lifted his burger, took a large bite, and chewed with his mouth closed while a glob of ketchup dribbled down the corner of his mouth.

If he'd been a different man—like his brother—she might be tempted to get up, lean toward him, and lick the ketchup off his face.

Life was playing tricks on her again.

Instead, she handed him a napkin and pointed at his chin.

"Something's wrong?" He wiped the ketchup from his face. "What is it? I'll take care of it."

She wrinkled her nose and shrugged one shoulder. "You don't want to hear about it."

"I'm a good listener."

"Really?"

"Ah, a skeptic." He leaned forward. "It's true. The

secret of my success with the opposite sex. The best aphrodisiac is just listening to a woman. Not trying to fix her, just listening."

She chuckled. "That sounds like you. I admire your honesty. It's too bad I'm not attracted to you."

"Shouldn't I get a consolation prize for making you laugh?"

"Sure." She held out her plate to him. "Have a fry."

He took one. "Worth the evening out. So what have you been doing since we last saw each other?"

"Your brother didn't tell you?"

"Tell me what?"

"That I'm in the same business as your family."

His brows slashed down, the easygoing enjoyment on his face wiped out. "A furniture company?"

She nodded. "So far, we're going custom. We're looking to acquire backing, and then we'll buy a plant."

He still frowned, his eyes narrowed as he pinned her with a fierce gaze that made her smile sweetly at him. "You might want to build the plant in a different city," he said, a hard edge to his voice. "I don't think there's enough room—or business—to fit another plant in this one."

She stared at him. With a half scowl instead of his usual genial smile, he looked harder and older. Like someone who had responsibilities. Someone who cared about his company.

"You didn't ask what kind of furniture," she said.

His expression didn't change.

She had to stop herself from rolling her eyes. "You're protective about your company. You surprise me."

"Most people are surprised, but I've grown up."

"You're more like your brother than I thought."

"I'll take that as a compliment."

"Then I guess it's okay to tell you that we make cat furniture."

His expression cleared, and he looked younger and carefree again. "No kidding."

"I'm as serious as a graveyard."

"I can think of some unserious things to do in a graveyard."

She groaned, and he laughed.

"The cat tables and ladder I saw in your living room?" he asked. "Did you make that?"

"My partner does most of the building. I do most everything else. We have more models that we make, plus we build furniture to spec. A client who lives in a loft condo with a high ceiling wanted us to build a tunnel of boxes for his cats that hang from his ceiling, and we just did that special for him."

"That's cool. I'd like to see it."

"You're serious? It's in my partner's barn right now. I can take you to look at it." A Maroon 5 song spilled out of the bar, and she waved her hand at the bar. "Unless you want to wait for karaoke hour?"

"Not unless you do. I can listen to karaoke singing any night."

"I was hoping to sing and watch everyone's horrified faces, but I suppose I can pass."

"We could do both," he said, grinning.

She laughed. "Finish your burger, and we can go."

"Done." He took out his wallet as she looked at his

plate and saw he'd eaten his burger already, only potato chips left.

"So you eat fast, too," she said.

The waiter stopped at the table with their bill and made a choking sound of suppressed laughter. Ryan shook his head, but his lips pressed together in a smile as the waiter left with his money.

"You're going to ruin my reputation," he said.

"You have a reputation?" She stood. "I've heard of guys like you."

"Your mom warned you against them?" He got to his feet, and they started walking along the sidewalk.

"My mother just told me not to settle for someone who didn't treat me well."

"I could treat you well."

"I'm sure you could." While it lasted, she thought.

"But you're not interested."

She frowned at him. "You know I'm babysitting for your niece, don't you?"

"Holden didn't mention it. I wonder why not." He grimaced, steering her to his parked car. "He knows we dated all those years ago. After you came to our grandparents' house for your book, he reamed me good."

His words made her feel warm inside and out. Knowing her cheeks must be flushing, she was grateful for the darkness gathering around them.

Some things she didn't want him to find out. Didn't want anyone to find out.

She got into the car, and he closed the door. Seconds later, he was in the driver's seat, saying, "He probably didn't want to remind me that you were still single. He wouldn't leave Cara with you unless he thought you could be trusted. He'd be afraid I'd corrupt you."

"I'm not that easy to corrupt."

"I know." He sighed dramatically. "To my deep regret."

As she shook her head, he pulled out of the parking lot. The windows were open, the weather was perfect, the man was witty and good-looking. She looked at him and felt sadness because he was not the right person....

And neither was she.

She could fix a lot of things, but that wasn't one of them.

12

"Hey, Sam, I'm on my way to the barn." Abby held her cell phone to her ear. "I'm showing a friend the cat furniture."

"Oh."

The one-word sentence didn't surprise Abby. Sam was better with her wood tools than words. But it was the tone she used, making it one word short of *oh shit*.

"You don't have to come out. I have the key. When we leave, I'll turn off the lights and lock up."

"That's fine, then." Her tone was normal as she said goodbye.

"Sam?" Ryan asked.

"Short for Samantha."

"I knew a girl named Samantha," he said.

She gave him a sideways look. "I'm sure you knew a lot of girls. Just drive."

By the time they arrived, it was night. A quarter moon shone down on them. About three-fourths up the driveway, it split into a Y shape. The left side angled off to the garage by the house, with the lights mounted on either side of the garage door on. The right curved to the barn, the lights off.

After they turned toward the barn, Ryan slowed the car to a crawl, and the tires veered onto the grass, off of the stone and gravel driveway. Abby, who'd been looking at the barn, glanced at him and saw his head twisted toward the garage.

"You're on the grass."

He straightened the steering wheel, gazing toward the dark barn. "I thought I recognized the car parked outside the garage."

She twisted to peer at the car. "It's not Sam's. Probably a friend's."

"Does the friend have a name?"

"I imagine she does."

"She?" He parked in front of the barn and looked at her inquiringly.

"She," she said, no hesitation.

"Huh." He looked at her, and she looked back. She didn't know how he'd caught on so quickly, but some guys were tuned into the nuances. She didn't say anything, just got out of the car. Sam didn't hide her sexual preference, but it was no one's business but hers.

With the lights off, it took a couple minutes to unlock the doors, step inside, and turn on the lights. A half smile of wonder spread on Ryan's face, as if he were a kid who'd stepped into Santa's toy factory. He walked around the barn, peering up and down and side to side. Checking out everything, from a ladder with a perch on each step, to a cat throne, to the walkway on top. Rubbing his hands on the different woods and the carpeted surfaces. Looking at the different cat pads and the patterns. Asking her questions about the designs. He even climbed up the ladder perch—shoeless, because Abby insisted he take off his shoes.

She laughed at him, and he laughed back at her.

Climbing down from the ladder, he asked, "How come we're not burning up for each other? We get along so great."

"Opposites attract," she said, but she didn't get it either. It would be easy to be with him. But instead, she was attracted to his uptight brother. His uptight, *engaged* brother.

Perhaps it was a way to pass on different genes to children. Or maybe her hormones were messing with her.

Ryan came to her side and slung his arm around her shoulders. She leaned against him, looking at the cat furniture for the second time that day. It was gratifying seeing it through his eyes, but it had been even more gratifying to see it through his brother's. Holden was harder to please, and when he was impressed, it meant something special.

"Why are you babysitting?" Ryan asked. "When you have this?"

She shrugged. "The usual reason. Money."

"Ah." He didn't say anything right away. Just stood with his arm around her. A peacefulness stole into Abby, and she could tell he felt it, too, his hold relaxed and his breaths even. He turned to her. "I could sell this."

"What do you mean, 'sell this'?"

He released her. Stepping in front of her, he swept his hand out to include every item in the place. "Your cat furniture. I know people who buy furniture. I'm vice president of marketing. I head the sales and the merchandising teams." He cocked his left eyebrow and shrugged. "It was Holden's idea. Turns out I'm good at it. I get along with people. They like me. Without me, the business wouldn't do as well."

"I believe you."

His eyebrow came down, and his eyes narrowed. "I could help you, too. Just drop a word or two here and—"

She put her hand over his lips. "Selling isn't the problem, it's keeping up. We need to hire people, buy equipment for Sam, and find a better place to make the furniture. We're supporting ourselves on this and even making money. But every time we start saving money, something goes wrong."

"Like what?"

"The roof." She peered upward. "It collapsed this past winter. Every piece of furniture in here was ruined. It all had to be redone."

"Wasn't it insured?"

She shook her head, her lips clamped shut. Not wanting to say anything against Sam, who'd been sick about the entire thing. "We were saving everything we could. Sam had to buy new saws, and she thought the roof would last at least until we could afford something bigger. And then we had all that heavy, wet snow...." Just thinking about it twisted her stomach.

He put his hand on her shoulder. "That's tough."

"A lot of people have it worse," she said with a shrug. "Sam and I have a plan. We tried to get an angel investor group to help us last week, but no one was interested."

"They're probably dog lovers."

Her humorless laugh turned into a series of choking barks. She clamped her lips together and shook her head. As if she could shake away every mistake and disaster, from the small to the big to the gigantic. Sometimes it felt like she'd made them all.

Lowering her hand, she took a deep breath before talking again. "We'll be okay. I'm going to sell my house, and we can use the money to see what we can finance. Maybe we can find a small plant somewhere. We don't even have to buy it; we can rent it. Start out small."

"Have you thought of going to Kickstarter?"

"We think we'd do all right on something like that, but not enough to get the money we need. It's more impressive to see at least a couple of pieces in person so backers can see the quality. And then show the brochure with the different designs. We can show our orders in the past year. We can show everything." She scrunched her face, because she felt scrunchy thinking about all the work ahead to find a new angel. Again. Just as it seemed the possible could happen, it became impossible.

"Two of the investors from the angel group wanted to invest, and three didn't." Her chest tightened. It had been so close.

He squeezed her shoulder. "Hey, it's tough out there. We're up against products made in Asia. It's not the slam dunk it used to be for us, either."

Taking a deep breath to open up her chest, she reminded herself they weren't the first to face adversity. Almost everyone did. Winners didn't quit. Winners kept going. They had to. If they gave up, the minute they quit trying and took that first step back, they became losers.

She nodded. "This is turning into a depressing date."

"We'll blame it on Aunt Daisy."

Her laugh sounded like it came from under water. Maybe that was it. While trying to save herself, she was emotionally drowning. "Daisy told me from the beginning that you wouldn't be perfect for me." She twisted from his loose grip on her shoulders. "Sam and I aren't giving up. It might take us another year or two, but we'll do it."

"Great attitude." He walked beside her to the door and waited while she turned off the lights and locked up. She felt embarrassed by the flimsy lock that any thief would be able to break.

In the car, he drove slowly down the drive. When they became even with the garage, he stopped his car and hunched down to look at the car parked by Sam's garage.

"Is that a BMW?" he asked.

"You're asking the wrong person. It's light gray and it's a car. I have no idea what kind it is unless I'm close enough to read the name."

"Good idea." He put the car in park, opened the door, and stepped out. Standing on the driveway, he stuck his head back in. "Stay here. I'll be right back."

Then he was off and running before she had a chance to say anything. Not even, *Watch out for the dog.*

He was almost at the driveway when the barking started. Loud barking for a big dog.

The next second, Abby had a chance to admire his agility as he turned and ran as if Cerberus, Hades' watchdog, was snapping at his feet.

She was on the driveway as he ran up, shouting, "Get in the car! Get in the car!"

Ignoring him, she held out her hand. "Treat! Loki, come and get your treat!"

As Ryan rushed around the rear of the car, she threw half an energy bar as far as she could away from Ryan.

Its mouth slavering, Loki changed course and chased after the treat.

"Get in," Ryan yelled as Loki found the treat and gobbled it up in a half second. "Get in while you can."

She ignored him again, crouching to catch the dog racing toward her. His slobbery tongue swiped her cheek, dripping saliva down her face and onto her top. Murmuring that he was her sweetheart, she hugged him and kissed his sagging jowls while he whined as if he was in ecstasy.

"Abby? Is that you?" Sam called from across the way.

She let the dog lick her mouth one more time before she stood, wiped her mouth with her sleeve, and threw the other half of the bar toward the house.

"Sorry for bothering you!" she called, seeing a tall, slender woman in the driveway, just at the edge of the light. "We're leaving now. Will you call Loki so we won't run him over?"

Sam shouted Loki's name, but he stayed another minute while Abby got into the car, finally leaving when she closed the door, and he was sure there would be no more treats. Only then did he gallop back to his mistress.

As Ryan steered slowly down the driveway, Abby said, "I bet that got your blood pumping."

"Not the way I was hoping to get it pumping," he said, but it was a throwaway line, his voice distracted, and she could tell he was thinking of something else.

A Michael Buble song came on the radio, and she sat back to listen, her mind drifting. Every day for her was full, but this was over-full. From purring cats to a slobbery dog, from one tamped-down brother to his too-loose brother. With a little girl who needed all the love Abby had to give, and yet she seemed to have some left over. Or at least something in a similar category to love, and she wanted to give it to the wrong man.

This was so...messed up. She needed to stop this.

One week and one day, and she would no longer see Holden. After next week was over, he wouldn't need her anymore. The sooner she stopped seeing him, the sooner she would stop wanting him.

"Your partner, Sam," Ryan said, "she's gay, right?"

"Excuse me? What about it?"

"No need to bristle. Just asking."

"And I'm not answering. It's none of your business."

He glanced away, his mouth flat. "I'm not so sure about that."

"An old girlfriend?" she asked.

"Something like that."

A cold feeling stole over her. It was cooler out now, and she wrapped her arms around herself. If she were Minnie, the fur on her spine would be raised, and she'd be watching out for trouble.

But she didn't have to look far. She suspected trouble was sitting right next to her, asking her out tomorrow night.

And she was saying, "Yes."

13

Ryan prowled Holden's office, reminding Holden of Abby's Quigley, the black one that didn't seem as smart as the older Minnie, who appeared to run the animal population of Abby's house. Even Abby and Grace seemed to understand her mews and jumped to accommodate her like well-trained staff.

Abby.

He couldn't get her out of his mind. Over the weekend, he'd been shutting down thoughts of her, but it was like chopping off a weed only to see another take its place. Now it was Monday; one more week where he had to see her twice every day.

One more week before he would return Cara to her grandparents. A thought that chilled him to his marrow.

"The meeting this afternoon." Ryan stopped in front of Holden's desk. "What's it about?"

"A new line of furniture." He held up his hand. He'd brought his sketches to their designer first thing Friday morning. "Suzie's working on it. We're going to use metal with some of the designs, or else wood with a metallic look. It will combine contemporary with traditional. We'll have to get an estimate of the costs before we make the final decisions. We'd like to start a couple key pieces in a month then see what kind of response we get. If it's positive, we'll go with the line."

"You didn't mention it to me."

"I'm mentioning it now. It's just going to be me, you, and Suzie." He studied Ryan's face—the slight frown, the lips curved in a dissatisfied downturn. "What's wrong? I thought you'd be all over this."

"It's not that. I have something else on my mind. Aunt Daisy fixed me up with someone on Thursday."

"You've seen her since?" Holden asked, grateful for the distraction from his thoughts.

"Yes. It's not serious. Turned out we already knew each other. But she's...interesting. And enlightening. And memorable. And something happened Thursday night that I've been thinking about ever since."

"That's four days of thinking. Your brain hurt from all that heavy work?"

"Real funny." Ryan shoved his hands in his pants pockets. "Actually, I'm thinking about a business opportunity, too. A new line that will fit in with what we have. Something different."

Holden sat back in his chair, his eyebrows up in a question mark. "Something you're creating?"

"Not me. I'm a people person." Ryan slouched onto the black leather chair in front of the desk. "The only creative thing I do is when I'm making love to a woman."

"Funny, the only one who's told me how good you are in bed is you."

"You're the funny one. There are legions of women who will praise my prowess in bed."

"Hidden legions. Does your new woman agree?"

Ryan's eyes narrowed. "Not yet. We're taking it slow. Slow is always better than fast. You and Portia probably know all about that."

Holden stiffened. "Leave Portia out of this discussion."

"You sure? You might learn something."

"Sure enough to throw you out if you keep it up."

Ryan snorted. "You wouldn't do that. It would cause too much gossip." He held up his hand. "But if it bothers you so much, I'll keep my mouth shut. Let's go back to the furniture."

"Okay." Holden sat back. "Talk."

"It's not the usual type of furniture."

"Different and unusual." A suspicion grew in Holden's mind. A foreboding. The way he'd felt driving last month when dark, mushroom clouds covered the sun, and the sky rumbled, then lightning flashed in the sky, taking out half the city's electricity for eight hours. "How different and unusual? What kind of furniture?"

Ryan thrummed his fingers on the arm of the chair. "I'm getting the idea you won't be surprised at my answer."

"Then tell me what it is."

Ryan's eyebrows contracted. "Cat furniture. But you knew that."

"And the old girlfriend you dated?" Holden heard the hardness of his voice, but he didn't feel hard. He felt numb, his emotions frozen. As if he knew what Ryan was going to say.

"Abby Pimm." Ryan's stare dared him to object.

"I wouldn't think you two were compatible."

"She's attractive, single, fun, smart, and talented. What's not to like?"

"You," Holden said.

Ryan howled with laughter. Holden's phone rang, and he picked it up, turning his head to hear his assistant over Ryan's loud cackles.

"Is everything all right?" Sherry asked. "There's a lot of noise coming from your office."

"I'm okay. Not sure about my idiot brother."

"I grew up with five of the beasts. Ignore them, and they'll eventually slink away."

She hung up before Holden could offer his condolences. Ryan was running down now, his guffaws turned into chuckles. His eyes bright, he leaned forward, ready to sell his idea.

"Look, you're worried we may have to lay off workers in the future. Didn't Grandma always tell us not to put all our eggs in one basket?"

"You know what Grandma would say about cat furniture."

"She liked cats."

"Because they killed mice. Everything in her life had to have a purpose."

Ryan's expression sobered. "You should watch out. You're becoming a lot like her."

Holden narrowed his eyes at his brother. "I'm not in a rut. I came up with the idea for the new line."

"Right. *One* line. Why just one? You're thinking small. Why not expand?"

"We're one of the most successful furniture manufacturers in the US. If Eagleton Furniture made cat furniture, people would laugh at us."

"As long as it pays off, why the hell should we care who laughs?"

Holden didn't reply right away. Laughter seemed like it was a long distance away from him, especially when he thought of Ryan and Abby together.

He ignored the twist in his belly. Ryan deserved to be happy, and Abby certainly did. Because of her, Cara was almost like other little girls. Even now, he still had to remember to speak softly when he was with Cara. If he used his normal curt voice, she shrank away from him, as if afraid of what he might do to her. But before Abby, Cara had been afraid to even look at him. He owed her for that.

A rock settled in his belly. He reminded himself that when Juliana's parents picked Cara up, she'd leave with memories she could cherish.

The reminder didn't make the rock go away; didn't even make it shrink.

"Tell me your idea," he said.

Ryan jumped up. "Abby and her partner have a backlog of orders, and they can't keep up. They only have one website, but they offer an associate's fee to other sites that send buyers to their site."

"So they get other sites to do the advertising for them. We do that, too."

"They have other ideas, but they can't implement them because of the production problem. They don't have a decent plant, just the barn workshop. Twice, they've been at the point where they were ready to invest in their own place. And each time, something happened that set them back financially. Meanwhile, other places are copying their cat furniture—" He stopped and shrugged. "You know the drill. The same way our designs are being copied."

"It's not the same thing."

"It sure the hell feels like it to them. Do you know how much Americans spent last year on their pets? Fifty-two billion. Most of it's on food and vet bills, but there's a market for this—a big one. And this is just the beginning. It's going to get bigger, and Eagleton Furniture can lead the way. We can be at the forefront. The leaders."

A buzz started in Holden's ears. "Are you saying we should *buy* the company from Abby and Sam then manufacture and sell their products? You really think Abby would say yes to that?"

Ryan grunted out a laugh. "No way in hell."

"That's what I thought. What do you think we should do?"

"Be partners in her business."

"You think she'll agree to that?"

The humor left Ryan's face, leaving it dead serious, for a second reminding Holden of their grandfather. "I think she has no choice."

"In that case, I'll say no."

"But, Holden—"

"Do you really want to put Abby in a position where she *has* to agree? When there's no other choice?"

"Not normally. But we'll do a better job with the products than they can. This is for her own good."

Holden groaned at Ryan, feeling a deep disappointment. "It's a funny thing. Almost every time someone says they're doing something for someone else's good, it's something that will benefit them."

Ryan's eyebrows slashed together. "We'll be taking a chance on her. We might not make any money from this."

"You're right, we won't make any money. Because we're not going to do it."

The muscles on Ryan's face tightened, and his blue eyes flashed, the way they had when they were kids—just before he attacked Holden with flying fists and kicking feet, enraged because he wasn't getting his way.

Holden held Ryan's gaze, not giving in. Slowly the tension eased from Ryan's shoulders. "I guess you're right. As usual." His tone sharpened with bitterness. "That must make you feel good."

"Not really. There might be more than one way to help her."

"Give her money?" Ryan sneered. "Don't you always say not to give your friends money if you want them to stay friends?"

"That's not what I meant." An idea had formed in Holden's mind, but he wasn't telling Ryan. He wanted Ryan to think about it and get the idea himself. It would be the only way he'd feel good about it.

But Ryan scowled and stomped to the door. As he reached it, he snapped around. "Have you seen Portia lately?"

Holden watched Ryan through narrowed eyes. Thanks to their upbringing, Ryan had two sides. The fun-loving Ryan, and the angry, resentful Ryan.

The angry Ryan didn't pop up often, but when it did, he could turn nasty.

"We had dinner on Saturday evening. We've both been busy and haven't had a chance to get together."

"Do you know what she's been busy doing?"

The hairs on the back of Holden's neck rose. "What do you mean?"

Ryan's mouth twisted in a smirk. "You like to give me advice. Fine, here's my advice back. Find out what your fiancée's doing."

Holden stared at him, not replying.

"That's all I have to say." Ryan whipped around and left, the door slamming behind him.

For seconds, Holden gazed at the closed door. Then, his movements stiff, he picked up his cell phone and pressed on a name, putting it to his ear instead of using the speakerphone.

The phone buzzed twice before Portia answered. She sounded the same as usual. No lilt in her voice or nervousness. Just her calm, smooth voice.

Eight days ago, he'd been pleased with their relationship, satisfied with their common goals and common sense.

That was before Cara. Before Abby. The last eight days had changed him—and he didn't know if it was good or bad.

"Are you busy tonight?" he asked. "Would you like to join me for dinner?"

"Um..." Portia's usually firm voice was hesitant. "I can leave early tonight. About seven? My place?"

"I'll have Cara tonight."

"Of course. I forgot. Your place is fine. I never did get a chance to meet Cara. I'll be there at seven."

"On second thought," he said, "I'll see if I can ask Abby to take care of her a little longer tonight. If there's a problem, I'll call. Otherwise, plan on me being there at seven."

They hung up, and he swiveled to frown at the blue sky outside his window. Portia had hesitated before accepting his invitation. Normally he wouldn't question her delay, but now he wondered why.

He picked up the phone to call the firm his company had used in the past to investigate background checks and items missing from the warehouse. But before the first ring started, he stopped the call.

Tonight he would ask Portia what was wrong. She would undoubtedly tell him, and everything would be fine.

Until then, he had one more call to make.

14

The phone's ring jerked Minnie awake from her nap on Mom's bed. She settled back down to sleep. Humans spent too much time talking to the phone. She wasn't quite asleep when another noise came to her ears. A fast padding of cat feet. She opened her eyes in time to see a black streak leaping through the air toward her. Quigley.

She didn't flinch. He wouldn't dare land on her.

He landed in front of her. *Did you hear the phone? It was Ryan. He's not coming tonight.*

Good. He's like the water. Mom is like the sun. She would go better with the earth than the water.

How can we find a man like the earth?

Holden is the earth.

I know that. Quigley nipped at the base of his tail before whipping his head back to Minnie. *But he has another woman. I heard Mom tell Grace.* Quigley's voice rose, excitement in it. *I know what we can do. We can scratch him and bite him and make him fall and hurt himself, and he'll have to stay here with Mom.*

If you bite him, he won't fall. He'll take Cara away and won't bring her back. Humans don't like being bitten.

Quigley jumped off the bed and ran out of the room. Minnie waited. In seconds, he flashed back into the bedroom, his fur ruffled. *Then you think of something better.*

Minnie stretched. Her body was older than his, but she was still in her peak. *I know what we can do.*

What?

The phone rang again. Her ears perked up, and she ran to the kitchen.

Because she didn't like her idea. Thinking of it made her feel funny inside. It could hurt her. It could kill her. She would only do it for the love of Mom.

She would wait to see if the humans would fix everything so she wouldn't have to do it.

———

One damn brother after another, Abby thought, picking up the phone in the kitchen. When Holden spoke, his voice was like dark chocolate. The kind that was a little nutty, a little rough-edged, which was strange, as he was so reined in. Strange because Ryan's was smooth, and he wasn't reined in at all. Every night, she'd had to warn Ryan to pull it back. She wasn't jumping in bed with him.

Or the back of the car.

Or her couch.

Or any other surface.

She suspected the challenge to make her say yes had kept him coming back.

But after tonight's abrupt phone cancellation, it appeared he'd tired of the challenge. He'd given up and was going after easier conquests.

Now, his brother...

If he really wanted someone, wanted her with all his heart, he'd be like a bull and keep charging until he conquered.

"Would you mind keeping Cara for a few hours tonight?" Holden asked.

"How few?" She gazed at the living room where Cara was making a monster puppet out of a kit that had belonged to Grace when she was a child. Last Tuesday, Abby and Grace had dug a box out of the attic, and every day, the three had played with it, she and Grace having as much fun as Cara.

"I should pick her up about nine."

"You have a date with Portia?"

He didn't answer at first. When he started to speak, she talked over him. "Don't answer, it's none of my business. I was just…" Feeling a little crazy? "Not thinking."

"Yes, I'm seeing Portia," he said.

"Tonight's fine."

There was silence for a moment. She watched Cara put a tutu on the puppet then balance a hardhat on its head.

"I hope it's not ruining your plans," he said. "Of course, I'll pay extra."

She wanted to tell him not to pay extra. That with tonight's date off and Grace sleeping over at her friend's house, she was glad Cara was staying with her.

And then there was the way she felt… Restless. As if the blood flowed too fast in her veins. As if a fire blazed through her body. She wanted to do strange things. To dance a flamenco. To tap her toes and heels. To swing her hips until every man on the planet looked at her with his loins stirring. And she'd look back, a flame in her eye.

She wanted to swirl. She wanted to feel heat. Not with Ryan. No, no, no. Just...with someone else. Someone who made her blood quicken.

She was feeling...odd. If Cara weren't here, she might get more than a little wild and do something very stupid.

"No plans," she said and heard her voice deepen. A voice like one of the mythical Sirens, calling to the sailors. *"Come to me. Come. I need you."*

"I have to go." She hung up, putting down the phone, her hand shaking.

She raised her hands to her cheeks, pressing her fingers against her cheekbones, feeling the heat emanating from her skin. This was craziness. Madness. She needed to take a bath in ice cubes.

Or better yet...

"Cara, you get to stay with me for tonight. Your dad can't come until—"

Cara's squeal stopped her. She jumped up and clapped her hands. "I get a sleepover!"

"No, sweetie, he was planning on picking you up. He—"

Cara's big smile and sparkling eyes fell into a downturned mouth and blinking eyes. Her shoulders slumped, her body drooped.

"But I'd love to have you sleep over," Abby said so fast the words practically tripped over each other. "Grace is at her friend's, so it will be just me and you."

Cara stood straight again. Not smiling yet, but hope radiating from her. Then she did smile. "It will be like you're my mom."

For an instant, Abby couldn't breathe, couldn't speak. So overcome with empathy and love for this small girl who didn't get any from her absent mother.

"I wish I was your mother," she said once again. Then she stepped toward Cara, and Cara ran toward her, and she fell to her knees, and they hugged. Her eyes closed tightly as the small girl's chin rested on her shoulder, the sides of their heads together. Abby smelled Cara's fresh scent, and love grew inside her, getting bigger and taller then expanding even more inside her. She wished she could wrap all the love around Cara in layers, thick and permanent, so she'd feel that love for the rest of her life. Wherever she was, whatever she was doing, she'd know she was loved.

How had this happened so fast?

Opening her eyes, Abby loosened her hold. The three cats and Lion sat around them, watching. For an instant, she wondered what they thought.

Probably that people were weird...and they wouldn't be wrong.

She kissed the top of Cara's head, much like she'd kiss Minnie, Quigley, or Lion. Pulling back, she put on a smile as if she were putting on a protective coating.

"I'll call your dad and ask him if you can stay over."

Of course he would say yes. He didn't deserve a daughter like Cara. He was better now than the first day when he'd been so rigid, but sometimes better wasn't good enough. Not when it came to children.

Abby pulled away from Cara, then she marched to the phone.

At least she wasn't sighing over him anymore. Right now, her hormones and her mind weren't singing the same song.

———————

He'd lost her. Holden pulled into the parking lot of a bowling alley so he could turn back to the city.

Before tonight, he'd never imagined he'd wait outside Portia's apartment to follow her like a suspicious lover.

But before tonight, he'd never imagined she'd be so nervous and jumpy, finally telling him that she wasn't feeling well. And when he asked, she told him she had PMS.

Normally, he would have believed her, kissed her on her forehead, and driven home.

That was before Ryan's cryptic warning.

So he'd parked his car across the street and just down the block from her condo building. After twenty minutes, he was thinking of leaving, when her silver BMW pulled out of the underground parking and turned the opposite direction that his car was facing.

He'd turned as soon as he could but ended up following the wrong car.

Stopping his car in the bowling alley parking lot, he called Ryan, who answered on the fourth ring.

"What do you know about Portia?"

"Nothing."

"That's not what you said."

"You know what?" Resentment hardened Ryan's voice. "She's your fiancée. You figure it out."

The phone went dead.

Holden sat in the parking lot for long moments before driving home, knowing what he had to do tomorrow.

But when he stopped the car, he wasn't at his home. He was parked in front of Abby's house, even though he'd given Abby his permission for Cara to sleep over. He'd driven here automatically, his mind working on the Portia problem. Keeping his hands on the wheel, the engine still running, he looked at the front of the house with the large front window. Through the filmy curtains, he could see outlines of a slight woman and a smaller girl.

They were dancing.

A sigh whispered through him. Tension rolled off of him. He turned off the ignition, pulled out the key, opened the door, and stepped toward the house.

15

"You're here!" Abby said, seeing Holden on her front porch. As if they were waiting for him. As if he was supposed to be here all along.

Instantly she felt like an idiot. "How come?" she asked, acting cool, as if she hadn't just made an ass of herself.

He didn't reply right away, looking dazed. She opened the door. "Come in. Are you okay?"

"I'm fine." He followed her into the living room. "Fine."

"You don't look fine."

"Daddy?" Cara peered uncertainly at him. "Did you come to see me?"

He gazed down at her, and in slow seconds, the bewilderment faded from his face. Blinking, he shook his head. It almost felt to Abby as if he'd just walked out of a thick fog and wasn't sure he'd ended up in the right place.

A purr caught her attention. Epic, the kitten who'd been so timid when she'd come to her home, was at his feet. As Abby watched, the kitten stood on its back legs and scratched his pants below his knees, getting his attention.

"Hey, here's my two girls." Speaking softly, he crouched and put one hand on Epic's head and one on Cara's shoulder. His expression still looked slightly dazed. "My dinner ended early, so I came here." He paused. "To see you and Epic."

Cara's face lit up, and a warmth kindled inside Abby. Then his gaze swept higher, wordlessly including her in the mix, and her body hummed soundlessly.

Not a good thing. A really stupid thing.

She told herself he was engaged. She told herself she was just feeling this way because it was a childhood dream. This was how her childhood had been before the accident. Mom, dad, her little sister, herself, and a kitten.

Stepping back, she told herself she wasn't a child, this was no dream, and he for sure wasn't a dream lover. Her dream lover would be smiling, laughing, kissing her all over. Adoring her.

She couldn't imagine this man who held himself so stiffly doing any of those things.

"Did you come to take Cara home after all?" she asked.

Cara gave a disappointed cry that sounded a lot like Epic when she objected to something. "We're doing a sleepover!"

"I want you to stay." Abby bent forward, her hands flat on the front of her thighs, her face level with Cara's. "I just wondered if your dad came here to take you home now that his plans have changed. I thought he might want to be with you."

"He can stay with us, too! He can sleep over." Cara twirled to face him. "You can, Daddy, can't you?"

His silvery gaze swept to Abby's and didn't leave. His eyes seemed to glitter, and she thought that when she met him five days ago, they hadn't glittered. Their silvery-blue color had been flat. Having his daughter with him, even this short time, had changed him. It had poked holes in the shell that surrounded him and kept away all emotion, as if it guarded his heart.

"Only if it's okay with Abby," he said.

She felt their stares on her as if they had weight. She saw the hope in Cara's face, as if she was wishing so hard, she couldn't breathe. And in Holden's, laughter and ruefulness.

And something else. Hope? Not as bright as in his daughter's eyes, but looking at him, she saw a spark. As if, for a long time, he hadn't had any and now he wasn't too sure, but he was open for the possibility.

She wasn't sure, either. All she knew for sure was that she had an oversized imagination.

And clearly it had been too long since she'd had sex.

"It's okay," she said.

Cara squeaked and jumped and clapped, her small face glowing, happiness streaming from her pores. "Abby's going to make popcorn! You can have popcorn with us. Where will you sleep? There's only two beds. Epic and I are sleeping on Grace's bed. And Lion!" She gave another hop. "Lion sleeps with Grace. Abby says so."

"She does?"

Abby shrugged. "We got Lion after the accident. Sleeping with him comforted Grace."

"It will comfort me, too," Cara said loudly, this girl who'd spoken so softly only a few days ago.

Holden gazed at Cara and swallowed, his Adam's apple working. Emotion, Abby thought. This unemotional man was swallowing emotion. Or it could be that his throat was dry, and she just wanted to think it was emotion.

"Daddy, you can sleep with us, too."

"It might be crowded," he said.

"Your father can sleep on the couch," Abby said. "Or the floor. His choice."

"I'll take the couch." He grinned at her. "Since I wasn't offered any other bed."

She cocked her eyebrow. He was flirting with her. In front of his daughter.

Her heartbeat fluttered. What happened to the uptight, stick-in-his-butt, slightly frazzled guy who'd come to her house a week ago?

And when did he get so...sexy?

He's engaged, she reminded herself. Maybe he flirted now, but that didn't mean anything. There'd been an attraction between them since the first day in her kitchen, even if she'd thought he was the opposite of fun. But that happened sometimes between men and women, and the best thing to do was ignore it.

She didn't admire women or men who took any pretty thing they desired just because they could. Not caring if it was right or wrong. She was not going to become one of them.

Even if she wanted it.

Even if he wanted it, too.

"There's always Lion's dog bed," she said.

Cara laughed so hard she fell to the floor and held her stomach.

She had a gift, Abby thought, grabbing on to joy so quickly. The speed of her recovery from years of lack of affection was amazing. And to see her like this... Abby's heart felt full.

A choking sound came from Holden, and she saw he was staring at Cara with astonishment. Abby's eyes prickled with moisture. Every time one of her foster cats was adopted, she always cried. Even for the ones who'd given her trouble. The ones who bit and scratched her and had bathroom accidents.

She'd been looking forward to the two weeks passing, but now she knew that when Cara was gone, she'd better make sure she had a full box of Kleenex in the house.

————

"Daddy, will you kiss me goodnight?" Cara pursed her lips to meet his as he bent over her bed. One peck, over quickly. She smiled at him, her face blindingly happy.

As he stepped back, the dog jumped on the bed and then the white cat, each settling down on a different side of her.

"You look like a princess in a fairy tale," Abby said, standing next to him, a faint scent of jasmine reaching up to him. "All you need is a tiara."

Cara giggled. "I feel like a princess. Will you kiss me, too?"

"Of course." She bent and hugged Cara, her whisper coming up to him. "You're a sweetheart."

"You're a sweetheart, too," Cara said, her voice clear. "This is better than any dream I ever had in my whole life."

"Oh, sweetie." Abby bent forward again and dropped a kiss on her forehead. "Close your eyes and go to sleep. I'll make eggs in the morning. Okay?"

Cara closed her eyes tight.

Holden had to force himself to follow Abby out of the room. All night he'd been unlike himself, as if his brain were still in that dark fog and only emotions pulled him through it. At the door, Abby turned off the light and murmured, "Sweet dreams."

She headed into the kitchen and offered him a drink. He surprised himself by accepting a beer.

"You're going to be a great mother," he said.

Sitting at the table, she gave him a look he couldn't interpret. He sat across from her. Even before she spoke, he could tell by the tension in her face that she wasn't going to tell him he was a great father.

"Did you know she hardly ever sees her mother?" she asked.

He took a sip of his beer.

"And apparently she sees her grandparents more often, but sometimes full days go by when she doesn't see them, either."

He didn't reply, though every word was a twist in his gut.

"Most of her time is spent with a series of changing nannies who spend most of their time on the phone talking to friends or texting them. The last one was sneaking out at night. She made Cara promise not to tell her grandparents that she left her alone in their wing of the house."

He closed his eyes, feeling as if he'd been kicked in his heart.

"You can't let her go back to them."

He nodded, looking at the ceiling and seeing a crack in it. Cara shouldn't live in a house with no love. And Abby and her sister shouldn't live in a house with a crack in the ceiling. "I know."

"You're going to keep her?"

"I have no choice, do I?"

"You have the same choice you did before. She told us she never saw you before her grandparents brought her here."

He lowered his gaze to her. She leaned toward him, her elbows on the table, her expression so serious and so hurt. As hurt and serious as he felt inside.

"How could you do that?" Her tone was low and tense. "It doesn't sound like you."

"I thought Juliana would take better care of her."

"You never checked. I can't understand that. It's crazy to me that you—" Her voice choked, and she set her lips together and stood. "Never mind. I'll get a pillow and a cover for the couch. You can watch TV. I think I'll go to bed early." She headed to the hall, leaving the full bottle of beer on the table.

Except for the pad of her feet and the hum of the refrigerator, there was no sound. She hadn't reached the hall when he finally spoke in a low voice that sounded tortured, unable to stop himself.

"Cara's not mine."

She turned, staring at him. She took a quick glimpse down the hall then strode back to the table.

"What do you mean?" Her voice was hushed.

"Juliana was cheating on me. Cara's not mine."

"You're sure?"

"By the time Juliana had gotten pregnant, we'd stopped having sex. She lived in California, and I lived in Wisconsin. We planned on getting a divorce, but my grandparents weren't in good health. I didn't want to upset them. Juliana was in love with her married boyfriend and in no hurry to end our marriage. When she found out she was pregnant, she begged me to wait until after the baby was born. Begged me to let her put my name on the birth certificate."

Emotions flitted across Abby's face: surprise, anger, sorrow. He braced himself for more questions about his marriage. Instead, she looked at him for a long moment before speaking.

"Does this mean you can't get custody?"

He laughed again. He should have expected the unexpected from her. "I'll get custody."

"Good. I wouldn't let a mouse stay with the grandparents."

"Who are upright, well-respected citizens," he said.

"I guess money can buy a good reputation," she said. "As many politicians have already discovered."

"I can't speak for politicians, but her grandparents aren't doing anything illegal. They aren't beating her."

"Not physically. But emotionally..." She sat, grabbed the beer bottle, took a slug then slapped it down. "Do the parents know she's not yours?"

He shook his head. "Juliana was afraid of what they would say. She made me promise not to tell them. In return, she promised a swift, uncontested divorce and said she wouldn't seek child support or any money, so I agreed."

"I suppose her parents were cold to her as well."

"I believe they were. Cara and Juliana had that in common."

"I'm surprised that Cara's so...lively already," she said. "But if she has to live with them again, it won't take her long to go back to the dark place. And now that she's known affection, it might be harder to go back to the coldness." Her tone softened. "I think you've gotten to her in time."

"Not me." He leaned toward her. "You."

She sat back. "I won't be part of her life. I was just doing this for two weeks. And you're getting married. Your fiancée will be her mother."

"Will she?" He took another drink before speaking. "Ryan hinted that he knew something about Portia. Something I should know before I marry her."

She put her hand over her mouth, partially covering it. He didn't have to be an expert in body language to know what that meant.

"You know," he said.

"I don't."

"You're lying."

She shook her head. "I'm not. I don't know anything for sure."

"Join the crowd." He held up his beer as if making a toast with it then brought it to his mouth and gulped it down, something he couldn't ever remember doing, not even as a teenager. He thumped the bottle on the tabletop, and she winced.

"Ask Portia," she said.

"I did. Are you going to make me hire a private detective?"

She closed her eyes, silent. Then her breath came out in a long sigh. "It's not just Portia. It involves someone else."

"Ryan."

Her quick laugh and crinkling eyes told him she was telling the truth as she shook her head.

"So you are going to make me hire an investigator?"

Her features settled into cool lines, and one eyebrow arched. "I'm not making you do anything. All I can say is that if you distrust her to such an extent that you're even thinking of calling a detective, are you sure you want to marry her?"

He didn't have to think about his answer. "No."

"No, you're not sure? Then—"

"No, I'm positive I don't want to marry her." As he said the words, a sense of freedom rose inside him. An exultation.

She tilted her head. "That was fast."

"I can be fast." He looked at her, suddenly filled with a deep longing. "Or slow." His voice turned husky. "I can be very slow."

She shook her head and laughed, and her laugh was husky, too. She stood. "I'm going to get the covers and a pillow for you."

"We could just sleep in your bed. Now that I'm not engaged."

"As far as Portia is concerned, you're still engaged. And tonight I'm sleeping alone." She grinned at him, and he saw a flush on her cheeks. When she walked away, he watched her hips sway.

It was going to be a long night...but it didn't matter. He headed to the living room and the couch, feeling lighter, as if a heavy weight on his shoulders had dissolved.

Tonight he should think about why he'd almost married someone so wrong for him, but with this bright, shining Abby sleeping so near to him, it was hard to think. He wasn't made of steel. And even the mythical man of steel had the hots for the inappropriate Lois Lane. The reporter who, if she discovered his real identity, would reveal it to the world.

It was probably a good thing that Abby had turned him down. He wasn't like Ryan, a rabbit that went after anything that wagged its tail his way. He wanted to be the eagle who had one mate for life, though it was too late for that, with one divorce behind him and engaged to another woman with secrets.

But that was in the past. He was looking to the future, and it felt to him that his forever woman was Abby, as if this knowledge was tangled in his DNA.

Only he'd once thought Juliana was his forever woman.

It wasn't that he didn't trust Abby, he thought. He couldn't trust himself.

Abby returned to the living room with her arms loaded with a pillow and covers. He took them from her, their hands touching, and his body reacting to that touch.

His emotions might be melting, but the rest of his body was not melting after all.

It was going to be a long night.

16

*W*hy are they sleeping in different rooms? Quigley
asked.

In the hall, between Mom's bedroom and the living
room, Minnie stretched. It was the time of the night
when the moon was the highest and the humans were
sleeping.

But as Quigley pointed out, not in the right places.
After all, Mom and Holden wanted to sleep together. She
and Quigley could smell it. Even Lion, sleeping as
soundly as the humans now, had smelled it.

They're humans, Minnie said. *They do things that
don't make sense.*

We should jump on top of him. Quigley peered into
the living room, where Holden stretched out on the
couch, breathing heavily in sleep. *Wake him up so he'll
go into Mom's room.*

*It's not that simple with humans. You never know
what they might do.*

I still think—

The bed in Mom's room squeaked, then creaked.
Sounds of her getting off it.

Minnie sat up, fully alert. Mom was awake. She did
that sometimes at night. Then she would sit on the living
room chair and take turns petting her and Quigley while
she read a book. Sometimes she put the book down and
just petted her. It was their time together.

A strangled yelp came from Mom's bedroom. Minnie and Quigley jumped up. As they dashed toward Mom's room, the mattress squeaked again; Mom collapsing onto it. Behind them, the couch creaked; Holden getting up.

It didn't stop Minnie. It was a fact that humans were slower than cats, and she needed to see what was wrong with Mom.

Quigley leaped on top of the bed before her, beating her by a head. But she came up after him and knocked him off. He yowled as he tumbled to the floor. She ignored him and craned her face in front of Mom's. Mom sat on the side of the bed, one knee up to her chest, holding her hands over her toes and saying bad words under her breath.

Heat streamed from her skin. Minnie liked warmth, but this was too warm for humans. Mom smelled of pain and confusion and something more.

She took another sniff, and she knew.

The mating scent. Even with her hurt toes, Mom wanted to mate.

Minnie put her paw on Mom's cheek to calm her, to try to take the hurt away, as Quigley pounced on the bed again, and running footsteps pounded on the hall floor.

Is she all right? Quigley asked. *Is she?*

She ignored him and continued soothing Mom with her soft paw as Holden burst into the room and flicked on the lights.

"Abby!" he called. "What's wrong?"

As if he didn't notice her and Quigley, he blundered to the side of the bed and leaned over Mom. Minnie hissed at him to stay back, letting him know she was handling it.

She didn't want him in Mom's room. He upset Mom. Men always upset Mom. She was better off without them.

Human females didn't seem to realize that males were only needed for impregnating them. After that, what good were they?

Not glancing her way, Holden put his hand on Mom's shoulder, his face close to hers. If he leaned a little closer, they would be kissing.

Instead of swiping her claws across his face, Minnie pulled her paw back as Mom gazed back up at him.

"I'm fine." She held a hand up. "Nothing to fuss about. My mouth was dry. I got up to get a glass of water and stubbed my little toe."

"Let me rub it." Holden didn't wait to be asked. He bent, took her foot in his big hands, and began to massage it.

Minnie approved. Massaging and petting were good.

There was silence for a moment, but Minnie heard their breaths quickening and their hearts beating faster. The mating smell thickened, coming from both of them, streaming out of their pores.

"I can bring you the glass of water," he said, and his voice thickened, too.

Her laugh was shaky. "My mouth isn't dry anymore. And I don't have a muscle cramp and really don't need a foot rub. It just felt too good to stop you." She jerked her foot away from his hands. "Thank you for the massage."

"It was my pleasure." He didn't take his gaze off her face.

She narrowed her eyes at him. "I should go to sleep now. So should you."

"It will be harder to sleep now," he said, and his voice softened. "I was dreaming about you when your shout woke me. Do you want to know what you were doing?"

"No!" Her breath sucked in. "Actually, I was dreaming about my parents before I woke."

"You're changing the subject."

"Sometimes the subject needs to be changed."

He laughed, but Minnie heard no humor in it.

"You never talk about your parents," she said.

"After my grandfather died, my parents sold their stock to me. They took the money and bought a home in Cannes. Every year, they vacation in Spain. They haven't been back since."

"Don't you or Ryan see them at all?"

"They call us on our birthdays." He made a motion with his hands, like he wanted something to go away. "I'd rather hear about your parents than talk about mine."

She stared at him for what seemed to Minnie to be long seconds before talking. "It's been nine years, and I still miss them. They were...the best. They taught me what parents should be like. And I wasn't the easiest kid."

"I don't believe that."

"Believe it. After all, I went out with boys like your brother."

He laughed, the sound low and intimate. Minnie hunched down to watch them. Next to her, Quigley did the same thing, keeping his mouth shut for once.

"And you're still going out with him."

"I don't think so."

"Because he canceled tonight?"

She reached out and put her hand on the side of his face. "I shouldn't tell you this."

Minnie's ears pricked up. Next to her, Quigley's ears perked, too.

They would have a lot to tell Lion in the morning.

The silence stretched as the two humans stared at each other. A movement broke the quiet, his hand cupping her face.

"I prefer you," she whispered.

His breath puffed out. "I'm still engaged."

"I know."

"Not much longer."

"Don't break the engagement over me." She made a sound that was either a laugh or a cry or both. "Not that I think you will. But just in case."

His lips curved slightly, and the next second they tightened to a line, all the softness gone. "I already planned on breaking the engagement. She's keeping secrets from me. It could be another man. I don't know." He took his hand from her cheek. "And it doesn't matter. Lately, I've concluded that I wanted to marry her because she's the opposite of Juliana, Cara's mother. Not because I love her or she loves me. We aren't passionate with each other. We're polite. We talk, but it's like talking to a friend who I don't really know that well."

"Ouch." She made a face. "In that case, you're doing her a favor by calling off the wedding."

"I'll tell her that." His lips curved up again, Minnie's sharp eyes watching every muscle of his face. "But this isn't about me, it's about you and your sore toe."

"My toe's not sore anymore, but I need to get up."

Minnie and Quigley leaped to the floor a second before he stepped back, giving her room to scoot out of bed. On her feet, she headed toward the bathroom while he strode to the living room and put his outside clothes on, the way humans did. Hiding their pale, furless bodies.

He should have climbed into bed with her, Quigley said. *He wanted to mate with her. And she wanted to mate with him. What's wrong with them?*

Minnie didn't have an answer. Many human actions were mysteries to her.

A sound from the living room that wasn't clothes being pulled on made Minnie pad silently to the entranceway. Peering in, she saw Holden take something out of his wallet and slide it into his pocket.

17

The tension seeped out of Abby, her tight muscles loosening as she stepped out of the bathroom into the hall. Holden waited for her, leaning against the wall, along with her two cats, his forehead creased with concern. All she'd done was stub her toe, but it was still nice to feel cared for, not alone. Everyone deserved that.

The hall light wasn't on, and perhaps it was a trick of the blue nightlight plugged into the bathroom, but they all looked...angelic. So beautiful her breath caught. Minnie and Quigley couldn't look anything other than the fabulous creatures they were, but even Holden looked like a fabulous creature tonight. Perhaps other women might think Ryan was more handsome with his golden looks, but she preferred Holden's strong jaw and chiseled cheekbones. And perhaps because he didn't smile often, when he did, it meant something.

"You sure you're okay?" Holden asked.

"I'm fine. You didn't have to wait, but thank you."

"I wanted to wait," he said, his voice firm, not taking any arguments.

She should insist that she didn't need his support, but she was feeling fragile tonight. Needy. Hungry.

"It isn't necessary, but I appreciate it." She tried to make her voice light, but it sounded shaky. Oh great, that was going to get rid of a man who had the caretaker mentality. She headed to the kitchen. "I'm going to drink some water then go to bed again. Don't let me keep you up."

She heard him follow her, her skin prickling, inside and out.

In the kitchen, she ran the cold water then lifted a glass from the cupboard.

"Your hand is shaking," he said.

Her back to him, she put the glass under the faucet, forcing the shivers to stop. When the glass was half full, she turned it off. Still facing the sink, she gulped down the water. Only then did she turn to him, her body chilled from the cold water. She wore a Springsteen T-shirt and blue tap shorts. Nothing sexy or sensual, but though he looked into her eyes, not allowing his gaze to drop, she knew she was turning him on.

Her body heated quickly. If only he wasn't engaged....

"I just got the shivers." Her throat tightened.

"You want to tell me about it?"

She suppressed a desire to laugh hysterically. She should tell him that she was shivering because he was engaged? She opened her mouth to tell him something light and funny instead, or even sarcastic and funny. Anything to hide her true feelings.

Only nothing came out. Not even a croak. Not even words that told him she was fine, and he should go to sleep in the living room, and she should go to sleep in her bedroom.

Instead she shivered harder, gazing up at him with what she knew must be a lost look on her face.

He stepped forward and took her in his arms, though she didn't want this. No, she didn't. No. She. Did. Not.

But perhaps it wouldn't hurt to take a bit of comfort. To put her arms around him. To lean against him and let him put his arms around her. To put her head on his upper chest, the top of her head just reaching his shoulder. To soak up his body heat. To have someone support her for once. To just hold on, hold on, hold on.

She reached up, her arms around his neck, and did all those things that it perhaps wouldn't hurt doing. And she'd been right, it didn't hurt at all. Instead it felt wonderful. She could let go of everything. Just lean against him and not think, just feel. Just hear the thump of his heartbeat. Just feel the warmth of his body. Just feel the hardness of his chest against her head. Just feel the erection pressing against her belly.

They stayed like that for moments before she reluctantly pulled her arms away. In slow motion, he unhooked his arms from her shoulders.

Below their waists, he drew away even more slowly.

She'd been warm a second ago. Now she shivered again.

"You're cold," he said.

"I'm fine." She stepped back. "Thank you for being here for me."

"It's my pleasure." His voice was rough.

"Well…" She forced herself not to look below his waist. Forced herself not to say, *"No, it was very much my pleasure."* Instead, she said, "I'd better go to bed."

He followed her. She stepped into the bedroom, her hand on the door handle, and twisted around. "I'm sorry for waking you. You can go back to sleep now."

"What if you get a nightmare?"

She laughed. "I don't have many nightmares. If I have one, I'll survive." She looked behind him at Minnie and Quigley. "My cats will wake me."

"They beat me to your bed."

"Minnie's a Siamese. They're very intelligent."

"She looks intelligent."

"And Quincy is very brave."

"I think he understands you. He's preening."

"I wouldn't be surprised. It often feels like they understand me. I swear they try to talk to me."

"I've never had a pet before Epic."

"You should get two cats. When you're away from home, they'll keep each other company. Epic won't be alone."

"It's not good being alone," he said.

"No." She should step back into the bedroom and close the door. She knew it. Yet here she stood.

And there he stood.

"I've been alone a long time." He reached out, and still she stayed. The tips of his fingers touched the sides of her cheeks. "I don't want to be alone tonight."

She closed her eyes, memorizing his touch. "Neither do I," she whispered. "But we shouldn't do this. Portia—"

"I can't marry her. I know that now." His fingers slid down to the hollow between her neck and her shoulder. "I've never wanted her the way I want you."

She kept her eyes closed. She heard the dull slap of his footstep as he stepped forward. She felt him against her again. Hard flesh and hard muscles and warm man.

"Don't send me away," he said.

She leaned against him for a second.

Then she lifted her head and stepped back. Hurt flashed across his face, followed by sadness then resignation. He started to turn.

"Come in," she said. "And close the door behind you."

———————

He shouldn't do this.

But when he'd held her, it had been like holding on to a fairy with warm blood running through her. Someone bright with possibility and hope. And it had been so long since he'd felt any of those emotions. So long since he'd even thought they were possible for him.

"You're a magic woman," he said.

She laughed breathlessly. "I'm not magic. I'm all too human."

"I'm human, too." He stepped toward her, afraid to say anything more that would show her how needy he was, how much he wanted her, the need pulsing through him. If she knew, he feared it would scare her.

"Wait!" She held up her hand. "Condoms."

He slid his hand into his pocket then pulled out his packet.

She laughed. "You must've won all the badges as a Boy Scout."

"My grandparents thought the Scouts were a waste of time. I wasn't allowed to join them."

Her forehead wrinkled. "I bet you wanted to join, didn't you?"

"Not as much as I want this." He slid the packet back into his pocket then took her in his arms.

She smiled up at him. "I've been told I'm very good in bed."

"I haven't had any complaints, but no one's told me that."

"I'll let you know if you deserve any merit badges."

———————

She wasn't wearing much, just a T-shirt and tap shorts, but he insisted on undressing her. Slowly. Very slowly. His hands and fingers skimming her skin.

Her eyes closed, her body heated, her breath quickened. They'd barely started, and already he deserved a merit badge for the first step.

"You can be my undresser any day," she said when she was naked, and he stood back, looking at her, up and down then up and down again, leaving her skin warm and tingling. Just like the heroines in the romances she read, she was melting a little inside.

"I didn't know that *undresser* was a job title."

"You could be the first. Women would pay you to undress them and look at them with hot eyes." Her voice lowered, and his eyes darkened. Watching them smolder, she felt strong, empowered, sensual. It had been too long since she'd felt this way, and she went with the flow, ready to see where it would take her. "I think they would pay you a *lot*."

"I don't think they would pay me anything. My eyes only grow hot looking at you."

She laughed softly, though she wanted to laugh loudly and with joy. But Cara was sleeping in the next room, and this would be a bad time for her to wake up. A very bad time.

"You're a true redhead," he said.

"Of course. And you're wearing too many clothes. Maybe I can torture you...er, undress you now."

He laughed softly, too, and tore off his clothes much faster than he'd taken off hers, not giving her a chance to try out her sexual torture. He'd folded hers and put them on her dresser, but he left his in a puddle on the carpet.

"Nice," she said, and he was better than nice with long, leanly muscled legs, flat stomach, and nice chest and arms. Muscled but not too muscled. She wasn't surprised he took care of his body, and right now she appreciated his care, as if he'd done it just for her.

"Just nice?" he asked.

She laughed again. This was a time of laughter. A time of loving. A time that she would want to remember again and again.

"Incredible." She raised her eyes to his face. "But why are we talking so much?"

He stepped toward her. "I've been imagining this in my mind, and I'm not hurrying anything."

Her body heat went up. If she had a fan, she would turn it on high.

Then he reached her. She had expected him to be thorough and methodical. She hadn't expected him to be slow and reverent. It started with a whisper of a kiss that made her demand more, their tongues meeting and dancing, their bodies touching, skin against skin.

Heat coiled deep inside her. Desire mushroomed and rose. Her legs weak, she clung to him as tremors started from just the kiss and just the embrace. A moan came out of her mouth, and she could hear the need in it. The want. As if it came from some secret, wild place.

"Yes," he whispered. "Yes."

And then she was on the bed while he sheathed himself in a condom, and she grinned. The Boy Scouts had missed a natural when his grandfather had kept him from the organization.

He joined her on the bed, and his hands and fingers feathered across her body.

Immediately, her body lit up. On fire. She couldn't stand it. Could. Not. Stand. It. She wanted more, more, more.

If she didn't have it soon, she would scream.

But she couldn't scream, not with Cara next door. Instead, small keening sounds came from her mouth.

"Stop," she said, her voice strangled. "Stop."

He stopped, and she immediately wished he hadn't listened to her. Her body throbbed and needed then needed some more. She wished he would keep touching her and would never, ever stop. But if he kept touching her, she would have to scream. Scream so loud she'd wake Cara, the cats, the dog, her neighbors next to her and behind her. And maybe even across the street.

"You're torturing me," she said, her voice throaty. "I want you *now*. I don't need foreplay, not this time. I just need you."

His eyes burned. "Not yet, just a little more." He bent forward, and his lips touched one breast, his hand cupping the other. And he touched and he kissed and he sucked up and down her then up again. And all she could do was hold her fists at her sides and try to keep her moans down.

"Next time," she said with a gasp, "I'm going to torture you."

He laughed softly. "Is that a promise?" His voice was like gravel.

She couldn't answer. He was torturing her neck now, and she had her arms around him, holding him, writhing under him and against him. Too much emotion inside her aching to break out.

And how did this man who she'd thought would be competent turn out to be the world's greatest lover?

"I'm ready," she said, her voice shaky. "Past ready. Now, please. Now."

He entered her in increments. Each one an agony. Each one an ecstasy. A long moan coming from her mouth.

And then he was inside her, and they were holding each other, the slow mating dance turning into a frenzy for both of them as they took more and more and more and gave more and more and more. Until she rocked against him, gasping, fireworks going off inside her.

Then he was clutching her, grunting as she held on to him.

Crazy, wonderful, incredible sex.

He waited until his pounding heart slowed before rolling off of her.

She stared at the ceiling in a stupefied, satisfied half daze.

"So how was it?" he asked, a lazy, satisfied smile in his voice. "Any awards?"

"A boatload," she said slowly. She felt like she was floating and didn't want to come down to earth. "The best I've ever had."

She felt his gaze on her, a warm weight. She turned her head.

"Me, too," he said.

She took his hand. "Will you stay with me tonight?"

"I'll have to get up before Cara wakes up."

"I'll get up to set the clock." She closed her eyes. "In just a minute."

"Okay," he said, as she felt her thoughts drifting away....

18

"**D**addy?"

His eyes snapped open, and he knew immediately where he was. In Abby's bedroom. On Abby's bed. Lying next to her. She was on her side, her back to him. He gazed over her shapely shoulder to see Cara looking from him to Abby with wide eyes.

He swore silently. At least a sheet was draped over their bodies. Pulling it up over their shoulders was the last thing he remembered doing before he fell asleep next to her.

The morning sunlight filtered through Abby's shades, giving Cara a clear eyeshot of them together.

Something slapped onto the bed. Quigley, walking between them. Holden inched back to give Quigley room. Abby's bed was full-size, and he was careful not to slide too far away from Abby.

A thought crept through his brain that next time they'd have to do this at his house in his king-size bed.

Minnie jumped on the bed and mewled a long sentence at Quigley in different tones and shapes. He made a growling sound to her, and it sounded to Holden as if they were talking about him and Abby and were not happy with what had happened.

He tore his gaze from the cats to Cara and noticed she was holding her kitten. As he wondered what the hell to say to her, the white cat leaped out of her hands. Now there were three cats on the bed.

The dog padded into the bedroom, too, and stopped next to Cara. The two of them looked as if they were posing for a portrait: a girl and her dog.

And he still didn't know what to say.

"Um..."

"Good morning, Cara," Abby said. "Oh, I like your top. Did you pick it yourself?"

She nodded. "My nanny took me shopping, and I liked this one."

"Great choice! Would you mind leaving the room while I get dressed? I'll come out real fast so I can feed Lion and the cats. Then I'll feed you and your dad."

Cara nodded and turned. At the door, she called Epic's name. Epic meowed then rushed out after her. So did the dog.

As soon as the door closed, Abby threw off the sheet and jumped out of bed. He held the sheet over him for a few seconds until he was sure Cara wouldn't return to the bedroom again. There was no way he wanted a six-year-old to see him naked.

"That was awkward," Abby said.

"What should I tell her?" He hopped out of the bed and took two fast strides to his clothes on the floor.

Abby grabbed a top from an older closet with sliding doors that ran the width of the bedroom. "Tell her the couch hurt your back, so you slept in my bed."

"That would be lying."

She gave him an exasperated look. "Then tell her what you want. In my opinion, some things are better for kids not to know. She'll figure it out when she's older. By then, she won't think any worse of us or be confused."

He pulled on his briefs then grabbed his slacks. "The couch was actually a bit uncomfortable, so it really wouldn't be lying."

She squeaked a laugh as she crossed to the door.

"Abby."

Reaching for the door handle, she turned slightly, her eyes meeting his.

"Last night was pretty wonderful for me."

"Me, too." For a moment, they stared at each other, and he felt his body respond to the way she looked with her red, messy hair, her face soft with satisfaction, her green eyes happy. Then she opened the door, turned into the hall and left him in the bedroom with the two cats staring at him.

"It's just you and me," he said.

Quigley headed to the door, but the Siamese talked to him while he got dressed. He had no idea what she was trying to tell him, but it was long and complicated, and he knew it was important. But he didn't speak Siamese, and he had some decisions to make. He wasn't looking forward to doing any of it, and he had the crazy idea that if he could understand what the cat said, he might make the right decision.

By the time Minnie and Quigley finished eating, Lion had gobbled his up moments ago and was watching Mom prepare the human food, poised to move fast if she dropped any morsels. Epic was still eating, and Minnie and Quigley reluctantly settled down on a sunny spot in the corner of the kitchen to watch the humans.

Cara carried plates to the table then hurried back to Mom. She laughed at something Mom said, happiness in her voice.

Everything is all right now, Quigley said.

Now they're happy, Minnie said. *But it's early.*

And they're humans, Quigley said. *Humans always make things hard. Why is it?*

I don't know. I think they want too much.

Even Mom? What do you think she wants?

Minnie didn't answer. She looked at Holden instead.

Holden was what Mom wanted. She could see it in the say Mom looked at him. The way Mom smelled when she was around him.

Minnie had talked to Holden while he'd put on his human clothes. Like most of his kind, he didn't understand her and couldn't reply. But she saw uncertainty in his face. And if he was uncertain, then Minnie didn't think he was good enough for Mom.

———

Not for the first time, Abby wondered what was wrong with men. What deficiency in their brains made them say and act the way they did? Even the best of them.

The first thing Holden said when he walked into the kitchen was that she didn't have to make breakfast.

"No problem," Abby said evenly, resisting the temptation to hit him over the head with the frying pan. "I'll eat the eggs myself."

"It's not that—"

"I told you, no problem." Her face heated, and she was aware of Cara staring at her with a scared look on her face. She forced a smile. "I was making an egg for Cara, too. Is that all right?"

Cara gazed at him with pleading in her eyes.

Watching her, Abby really wanted to kick him in the shins. She wasn't normally an angry person, but she was not immune to the emotion and was getting pissed off now.

"That's fine. I didn't mean—"

"Great!" Abby crouched in front of Cara. "Sweetie, I bet Lion would really like it if you threw a ball for him until breakfast is ready. Okay?"

Cara nodded, but her face didn't light up as it usually did.

Abby thanked her then stepped to the silverware drawer. Only when the screen door clicked shut did she turn to Holden.

He looked miserable. Good.

"You've got this all wrong," he said.

She crossed her arms then uncrossed them, making an instant decision that she was not going to be that bitter person. Just because they were good together in bed didn't mean anything.

"Don't make excuses. I don't need them; I don't want them. You've got the morning regrets written in giant letters on your face. I'm okay with it." She shrugged. "We had a good time. It doesn't mean anything."

"That's not it. It's just that..." He rubbed his hand through his hair. "There's Portia. I should take care of that first."

"Don't take care of it on my account." She shifted to the stove, turning the heat on to medium. "Would you mind setting the table? In a half hour—"

A hand on her shoulder stopped her. "It was more than a good time in bed," he said, his voice raw. "I'm not having the morning-after regrets. I just feel...dishonorable doing this while I'm engaged."

She turned and looked into his eyes, so close to her, so troubled. She sighed, letting go of the remnants of anger. Not asking him where these thoughts were last night, because she knew it wasn't just him. There'd been two people in her bed. She hadn't wanted to make love with an engaged man...but that's what she'd done.

"Neither of us made any promises last night. Let's just eat."

Before he could object, Cara returned, and the eggs were done. Holden ate breakfast with them after all, and Abby focused her attention on Cara, getting giggles and smiles from her. Even Holden was smiling at the end when he left, squeezing her hand and saying he'd call.

Then they were gone. She closed the door and leaned against it. Only then did she lower her eyelids and let herself wallow in sadness for a moment.

And another.

And another.

Her instincts were normally right, and when he'd walked into the kitchen, she'd seen the what-the-hell-did-I-do look in his eyes. He could pretty it up all he liked, but she'd seen what she'd seen, and she knew what she knew.

She sucked in a deep breath of air and headed to her office and turned on her computer.

Like a million other women who'd thought, *This man is different,* she'd been wrong. So what? Too bad. She'd get over it. It was his loss. She was a wonderful lover. She was a wonderful person.

But, oh God, it hurt so bad.

The computer loaded, and she stared at it for a long moment, just feeling the ache of rejection. The ache of a bruised heart. Wondering how she could have misread him so much.

Maybe he was one of those men who, once they had something, didn't want it anymore.

She was better off without him.

After all, they'd only known each other for a short time. For whatever reason, her body had zeroed in on him and said, *This is him. This is The One.*

But her body was wrong. Because The One wouldn't be sorry after the most wonderful lovemaking in his life.

Her emotions numb, she opened her email. It was either that or curl up and cry, and she'd done enough of that in her life already.

She deleted the first three emails from places trying to sell her things and sent another one to spam. The next one said "Angel Investor," sent by a man whose name she vaguely recognized. She read it, but the words didn't sink in, her mind numbed along with her heart. She read it again, and still nothing. The third time, the words finally got through to her mind. She blinked and read it again. Then a fifth time to see if it really said what she thought it did.

Oh God. Oh my God.

She put her hand to her mouth.

Oh God, oh God, oh God, oh God.

She picked up the phone and pressed a familiar number.

19

Ryan came into Holden's living room with his I-know-I-was-bad-but-I can't-help-it look and three puzzles for Cara. Holden crossed his arms and listened to her thank him with her small voice as she stared with rapture at the puzzle with the princess, castle, rainbow, and unicorn. All it was missing was a kitten, but she had her own live one and didn't need one made of layers of cardboard.

Still in his generous-uncle mode, Ryan helped her open the box, telling her it was a floor puzzle. As she dumped the pieces on the rug, Ryan turned to Holden.

"Beware of Greeks bearing gifts," Holden said.

"Hey, it's a unicorn, not a Trojan horse. And we need to talk."

"Maybe you need to talk. Not sure if I do."

"Yeah, you do. We're all the family we've got."

Holden opened his mouth to answer him when the lack of movement on the floor caught his attention. He swung his gaze to Cara. "All three of us are family. And one kitten."

Beaming, Cara turned back to her puzzle pieces.

"Cara, Uncle Ryan and I will be in the kitchen." He nodded at the kitchen she could easily see just by turning her head.

"Okay, Daddy."

In the kitchen, Ryan opted to stand a few feet from him while he made coffee, telling Holden that someday he was going to be a great dad. Each word was like broken glass rubbed onto Holden's nerves.

Only a short time had passed since Cara had been dropped off at his house. He'd never been an emotional man. He'd only taken Cara because it was the right thing to do. Because her grandparents were running away from her as if she carried the plague.

And now taking care of her seemed to be the most important thing in the world that he should do.

He set the two coffees on the kitchen island. There were stools on the other side, but he remained standing, and so did Ryan.

"What do you want?" Holden asked.

"To apologize. I was an ass yesterday."

He gazed toward the living room. "You were. I accept your apology." It was easy to forgive him when he'd done something so much worse.

And so much more wonderful.

"Don't make it so easy. I don't deserve it."

Something in Ryan's voice—maybe it was sincerity or just a good imitation—caught Holden's attention. He looked Ryan straight in his eyes. "You want the truth?"

His forehead scrunched, Ryan looked down at his shoes then up. "Like the movie says, I don't know if I can handle the truth. I've been pretty much a shitty human being."

"I don't know if you're that far gone, but you've been selfish. You feel entitled."

Ryan raised his gaze. "That's the difference between us. You think every person is entitled."

"You're wrong there. I think everyone has to earn it. Even me, even you."

"How?" Ryan frowned at him, not an angry frown but as if he really wanted to know how he could earn his entitlement.

No, Holden thought, this wasn't about earning entitlement for Ryan. He wanted to know how he could earn respect.

"It's simple but not always easy. By being a decent person."

"Let me give you a scenario." Ryan took a gulp of coffee before continuing, and it looked to Holden like he wished it was a slug of something alcoholic. He set the mug down. "What if your parents were selfish shits? What if the grandparents who raised you didn't like anything you did and kept comparing you to your older brother? And then you grew up and grew a little wild and were careless and uncaring. And no one was surprised. They all expected it from you, and you sure the hell didn't blast their expectations. How hard would it be for that guy to turn into a decent person?"

"I don't know. You tell me."

"I can't."

"You're the only one who can. I'd think in that case, you'd want to show the world you're not letting people who were lousy at child raising define you. That you're a hell of a lot better than what they or anyone else thinks."

Ryan turned his gaze to the living room. "But what if you're afraid you're not?"

"You think everyone isn't afraid?" Holden made his voice low when he wanted to shout at Ryan. But not with

Cara in the house. "You think everyone doesn't have doubts? You think I don't? If you do, you're wrong. I'm loaded with doubts. Ask any psychiatrist about self-doubt. They'll tell you the only people who don't have them are psychopaths."

Ryan looked at him again with a half grin. "So by doubting myself, I'm proving I'm not a psychopath?"

"As far as I know, you could still be a psychopath. But going forward with your life despite the doubts proves you're going to keep trying until you get it. Just like the rest of us."

Ryan nodded at the patio. "It's looking good outside. You mind talking on the patio?"

Holden picked up his coffee and raised his voice so it would carry into the living room. "Cara, Holden and I will be on the patio in the back."

"Daddy, I got the rainbow!"

He frowned at Ryan. "You go ahead. I'll join you in a minute."

He was glad Ryan didn't follow him. Ryan would think he was doing this out of duty. Or out of pity. Maybe that's what had started it, but now he was doing it for the same reason Cara had lost her heart to the kitten. Epic needed her. Cara needed him.

There was something powerful about being needed. It was hard to walk away from that need, hard not to lose your heart.

He took a moment to admire the rainbow and Cara's beaming face. Then the kitten batted the puzzle pieces out of order. Cara turned to scold Epic, and Holden told her he'd be on the patio, in case any more kittens attacked her princess castle.

He left to her giggles, and though he knew taking on the role of a father was going to hold challenges and irritations, right now being a father just made him feel...pretty damn great.

And then he thought about the rest of his life, and that great emotion drained away.

Everything Ryan had talked about pertained to him, too. The reason he was so stiff and held in his emotions. Even after last night.

He'd never been loved as a child, and that ruined him for love. He made wrong choices, choosing women who couldn't love him back.

And what if he'd done it again?

Just about to step onto the patio, he stopped, fear shutting down his breath.

"Something wrong?" Ryan pushed out of the cushioned rattan chair.

Not able to talk, Holden shook his head and stepped onto the patio. He forced himself to exhale and inhale. To push down his own self-doubts and concentrate on Ryan. "What's this about?"

"Portia," Ryan said.

Holden headed to the patio railing. The grass sloped to the lake below. It was a perfect day, the sun not too hot yet, the air dry enough that there were no mosquitoes, just the buzz of flies. Later on today, he would do something outdoors with Cara, but he didn't know what that should be. He wasn't used to being a parent.

He didn't want to talk about Portia. He didn't want to think about her. But she was like a wisdom tooth that needed pulling. Better to pull it out fast.

After that, he would have to talk to Abby, but Portia first. "What about Portia?" he asked.

Ryan came up next to him and leaned his arms on the railing. "A few nights ago, Abby took me to the old barn where her partner makes the cat furniture."

"That's not news. I thought you were going to talk about Portia, not Abby."

"I'm getting to it. Now who's the impatient one?"

Holden raised his eyebrows. "We're arguing about this, too?"

"It's a story. Stories have to unfold."

"I don't want a story. I want facts. I want the truth."

Now it was Ryan's turn to look at him with his eyebrows raised. "Our lives are stories. And what's a fact to you is a lie to someone else."

"I don't know what the hell that means."

"That's because you see life as black and white. I see it in colors."

Holden thinned his lips. There was truth in what his brother said. There was also bullshit. "Go on with your story."

"So you know the set-up of the place," Ryan said. "The driveway splitting up, with the house and garage on one side, the barn on the other."

Holden nodded.

"Thursday night, it was dark out, and there was a quarter moon," Ryan continued. "The house was dark, too, but there were lights on by the garage, and I recognized a silver BMW parked on the driveway."

Holden's shoulders and neck muscles tensed.

"I already had the impression that Sam was gay," Ryan said. "I asked Abby about it, and she didn't say she was but didn't say she wasn't."

"Did you ask who Sam's guest was?"

"Would I do that?"

"Yes."

Ryan huffed a laugh that didn't have any humor in it. "You know me too well. Abby said she didn't know, but I had the feeling she recognized the car."

Holden's hands clenched.

"I think it was—"

"Portia and Sam were sorority sisters." Holden stared at the ripples on the lake and the sunlight sparkling on the blue waters, as if the sight saved his humanity. "She told me they were having dinner together."

"I see." Ryan pushed away from the rail. "I suppose it doesn't mean anything."

Holden nodded. But in that case, why were the house lights dark? And why hadn't Portia told him she'd gone to Sam's house? And if Ryan's suspicions were right, it would explain Portia's reluctance to have sex. It would explain a lot.

He'd already made his decision to break their engagement. This should make it easier.

"I'd better go," Ryan said. "I have a date this afternoon. And there's a cute blond in the family room whose artwork I need to admire. See you later."

Listening to Ryan's footsteps walk away and then the click of the door, Holden wondered who his date was.

The last woman he knew Ryan had dated was Abby.

A chill went through him, his stomach twisting.

———————

Grace came home, and Abby screamed her news. "We've got an interested angel!"

Grace's mouth opened in an O. She dropped her overnight bag, her eyes wide. "For the business?"

"I'm not talking about a trip to heaven."

Grace squealed. Abby squealed. They grabbed each other and jumped like two young girls.

Abby pulled away, still holding Grace's shoulders and Grace still holding hers. "It's not set yet. He wants to see the workshop and talk to me and Sam."

"Call him and set the date," Grace said, her voice high.

"I've been trying to call Sam for two hours." Her voice was high with excitement, too. "She's not answering the phone or her email."

"Go to her house."

"I will." She squealed again. Grace squealed, too, then they danced around the house. Minnie and Quigley leaped onto the cat tower to stay out of their way, Minnie scolding them loudly, voicing her disapproval of their wild laughter and noise.

After two more dance circles through the house, they flopped onto the couch, dizzy and grateful and breathless from the laughter and happy dancing. Abby felt boneless. She felt wonderful.

First the sex with Holden, and now this.

It had to work. It just had to.

Her heart still hammering, she jumped to her feet. "I'm going to try Sam again."

"Maybe she's working," Grace said. "If she's using one of her saws or has her music blasting, she wouldn't hear you."

Abby nodded, though this last week, she was pretty sure it wasn't work that was keeping her business partner busy. But she wasn't telling Grace what it was. Just as she wasn't telling Grace what she'd done last night.

Some things weren't any of her little sister's business.

Of course, if Grace became sexually active, that would be different. Grace would need to tell her everything.

Abby just hoped that didn't happen for a long time. Grace was much too young.

"If she doesn't answer," she said, "I'm going to drive to her place. She needs to be there when the angel comes. He said he's done woodworking projects, and he'll probably have questions for her."

"I'm going to crash." Grace pushed up from the couch and yawned. "We talked most of the night, and I can sleep for hours."

"Dream that the angel loves our work and wants to fund everything," Abby said and hurried to the office.

———

Twenty minutes later, she was pulling into the driveway of Sam's farm. She recognized the silver BMW parked by the garage. Portia's car.

Her shoulders tensed, though the car parked outside the garage was making it easier not to feel guilty about last night.

The front door was open when she reached it, just the screen door keeping her out. Before she could knock, Sam's rottweiler/boxer mix rushed to the door, barking ferociously, teeth showing. Abby put her hand to the screen for the dog to smell.

"How's Loki?" she asked. "How's my sweetheart? I don't get to see you enough."

Behind him, she saw three cats. Loki was great with the cats, but he hadn't been allowed in the workshop since the first week they started their business, when he'd chewed up a cat ladder and two cat perches.

"Hi, sweeties," she said. "Is your mama home? Huh? Will one of you get your mom for me?"

They looked at her, nowhere near as talkative as her cats. She wasn't surprised. She'd always known her cats were exceptional.

She rang the doorbell, getting more wince-worthy barks from Loki that scattered the cats. She finally shouted Sam's name through the screen, adding, "It's good news! Get your ass out here so you can hear it."

"I'm coming!" Sam yelled, the shout coming from the back of the house.

It took two minutes before she could see Sam coming to the front. She wasn't alone. Portia padded behind her. With her sleek body and dark brown hair, she reminded Abby of a beautiful feline.

The sound of tires crunching over gravel made her look behind her. She recognized the car coming up the driveway, and she groaned.

"What's so important?" Sam asked, opening the screen door.

"I've got good news." Stepping inside, Abby looked at Portia. "And I've got bad news."

20

It looks like everything is going to work out, Quigley said.

Minnie lifted her head from the pool of sunlight she and Lion shared on the sofa. Quigley was at the top of the ladder, even though his obsession to be on top was depriving him of the direct rays of light.

Why do you think that? Minnie asked.

Mom is getting the money she needs, and she even has a mate.

We talked about this before. These are humans, and nothing is that easy for them.

But Mom isn't like other humans. She's better than them.

Exactly. Minnie put her head down.

Quigley leaped down the ladder, perch by perch, until he reached the carpet. He sashayed up to the couch and jumped onto it.

Minnie let him know with her stare and the lifted fur on her back that he was not getting her patch of sunlight. It was enough that she was sharing it with Lion, but he'd been there first. Besides, he was too big to push off.

I get it. Quigley stopped by her back paws. *You're saying it's the other humans who might mess things up.*

You are so smart, Minnie said.

I am. Quigley bent to lick the fur on his upper chest.

Minnie lay her head down again, the back of her head against Lion's side. He made a nice pillow.

What if it doesn't work out for Mom? Quigley asked.
What are we going to do then?

I told you before. We'll have to fix it.

Lion raised his large head. *How?*

She closed her eyes. The problem with Quigley was he didn't believe her. Quigley had to see it to believe it. And Lion would tell her to leave it to Mom to fix.

Lion didn't know humans like she did. He'd come to Mom as a rescue like her, but he'd been with a family before that. He'd never been on the streets, hiding from predators, dodging cars, looking for scraps to eat.

Quigley didn't know what it was like, either. But if the time came to act, he would have to follow her, and together they would see what would happen.

And if he didn't follow her, she would have to fix it herself.

———

Abby's SUV was parked next to Portia's BMW.

A dog was barking in Sam's house.

Holden marched to the front door. He wasn't letting anything stop him.

It took a moment before the barks stopped and the door opened. Abby invited him inside, her eyes sad, her lips twisted in a grimace.

Behind her, Sam scowled at him. She stood in front of Portia as if she was protecting her, though she was oddly leaning to the left. Then a low growl came from her thigh level, and Holden saw she was holding back a large, drooling, growling dog that seemed ready to pounce on him.

"Did you come to warn them?" he asked Abby.

"I had no idea you were coming here." She frowned. "Where's Cara? Is she in the car?"

His tension eased. Of course she hadn't known he was on his way. If anyone should feel betrayed, it should be her. He'd made love to her when he was engaged, even though in his mind he'd been free.

And thank God, he would soon be free.

"Don't worry." He wanted to reach out and tell her everything was okay, but it wasn't the time. Not yet. "Cara's with Daisy."

She smiled at him, and it felt like the sun coming out. He wanted to bask in it but couldn't. Not until this was over.

He turned to Portia. He needed to get this done. "Do you have a few minutes?"

Sam bristled. "Anything you have to say to her—"

Portia's hand on her shoulder stopped her, and she stepped around her protector. "I need to do this."

"Do it where we can see you," Sam said.

"Holden won't hurt her." Abby stepped to Sam's right side and took her arm. "Let's go into the kitchen."

Sam narrowed her eyes at him then snapped around and stomped into the kitchen with Abby, dragging the dog with them.

With everyone gone but three curious cats, he could see that the room had about a half dozen pieces of cat furniture plus one wider and longer cushioned perch that must be for the dog. In this odd, rundown farmhouse, Portia looked as out of place as a gazelle in a lion zoo.

"Why did you accept my offer of marriage?" he asked.

"It's complicated."

"Life is complicated. Sex isn't. Or it shouldn't be."

Her lips twisted. "That's where we differ."

"So you're bisexual?"

Her lips tightened, then the stiffness oozed out of her. With a sigh, she shook her head. "I'm gay. And I'm sorry I didn't tell you. Very sorry. I knew how disappointed my parents would be with my choice, but that wasn't the only reason. I wanted children."

"You can be gay and have children."

"You're right. I'm still not being honest. The truth is, I wanted to be normal." She shrugged, her eyes and mouth unhappy.

"The only normal people I know," he said, "are ones who I don't know very well."

She frowned at him, and he realized she didn't get the subtext, and he needed to explain.

"As soon as I get to know them, I see their quirks and oddities." He looked straight into her eyes. "No one is normal."

"You're being kind." She grimaced. "I suppose I should thank you, but to be honest, our engagement is partly your fault. When you asked me to marry you, I knew you didn't love me. In fact, I could tell you didn't have any strong feelings for me. You just thought I would be a good wife." She raised her chin. "My parents were well-off. I looked like the woman you should marry. I wasn't going to embarrass you like your first wife did. I would be a conscientious mother. And I would never cheat."

"I was wrong in the last instance, wasn't I?"

"But not the others." Her mouth tightened, her only sign of discomfort. "And I'm sorry about the cheating."

"Don't be." After all, he'd cheated, too, though he wasn't going to tell her. He didn't want anyone to think less of Abby. "You're right about it being partially my fault. I'm glad we both found out now before we married. I think we can call off our engagement."

"Yes." She pulled off her engagement ring and held it out to him. "Here."

He folded his fingers around it, the four-carat diamond digging into his palm. "Will you have trouble canceling the arrangements?"

"Since our wedding was scheduled for October, we should be all right." She shook her head. "And please, don't offer to pay for anything. I should never have agreed to your proposal. In the end, I don't believe I'd have gone through with it. It's an expensive lesson, but I can afford it."

He nodded. "What we can't afford is to ruin our lives."

She held out her hand. "Thank you for being so..."

"Kind," he finished for her.

She laughed and instead of shaking his hand, leaned forward and kissed his cheek.

He stepped back, glanced behind her. Of course, Abby didn't appear. She was in the back with Sam and Sam's attack dog. He couldn't stick around here now. He'd have to go to her house later, tell her he was free, and they could have a relationship. She could be with Cara during the day. At night, they could be together and take it from there. Take it slowly.

He would see if she would still want him once she knew him better.

This time, he wasn't going to make snap decisions. For a deliberate man, he'd made two very bad decisions in his personal life. He couldn't take the chance of doing it again. Especially now that Cara might be hurt as well.

Though he could swear that Abby was the most genuine person he knew over the age of ten, he was going to date her for a long time before making any commitments.

———

"It's an odd day," Abby told Grace.

"There are so many of those." Lying next to Abby on a blanket spread on the sand by Angel Lake, Grace announced this with all the drama of a diva—or a teenager. And despite all the ups and downs of her day so far, Abby had to hold back a laugh. Teens were so dramatic.

Besides, the sun beat down on them. Boys were watching her sister in her blue bikini. A few men had ogled Abby, too, though most of them were with their families or too young for her.

None of them made her heart beat faster. Only one man did that.

"What was wrong with the angel's mom?" Grace asked.

"He didn't say. I think she's sick."

"I hope not," Grace said. "For your angel's sake, of course, but ours, too. If his mom dies or is in serious trouble, he'll be grieving and won't want to think about investing in your company." She sighed dramatically. "Do you ever think that God doesn't love us?"

Abby stared at her. "Don't even say that. Sure, not everything will come together, but that's how life works."

"How it works for *us*." Grace's lower lip pouted, and Abby's belly tightened.

"Don't talk that way. It's how it works for most people. Life is like one big puzzle." She gestured widely. "With millions of pieces, and no box top with a picture to show you how to put it together."

"So with every piece, we've got to figure out how it fits in?"

"Pretty much."

"And I'm supposed to spend my life putting pieces together." Grace wrinkled her nose as if something smelled bad.

Abby resisted an urge to hug Grace. A hug on the beach would embarrass Grace. "No, you're supposed to spend your life enjoying as much of it as you can. And loving as many people as you can."

Grace stared at her, and Abby laughed shakily, tears springing to her eyes. "I don't know where that advice came from. I think I'm channeling something from our mom. She's sending words of wisdom from heaven."

Moisture gleamed in Grace's eyes. "It's not Mom. It's you. That's something you would say."

"Really? Guess what? This is definitely something Mom would do." And she looped her arms around Grace's shoulders and hugged her tightly. With a laugh that sounded a lot like a sob, Grace hugged her back.

Grace's skin was warm, and she smelled like sunscreen and sunlight.

When they pulled apart, Grace wiped away tears, and Abby sniffed and blinked her tears away before they fell. Then she shook her finger at Grace. "And when I say 'loving many people,' I don't mean sex."

"Abby!" Grace rolled her eyes and put her hands over her ears. "You're embarrassing me."

"Good. That's my job." She stood, aware of gazes on her. She sucked her stomach in. "I'm hungry. Let's go and eat dinner."

"Can we order pizza tonight?" Grace grabbed one corner of the blanket; Abby grabbed another.

"I can make pizza," Abby said.

Grace frowned then smiled determinedly. "Your pizza is always awesome."

Abby took the blanket from Grace and folded it herself. The least she could do, since Grace lied about her pizza, which was nowhere near awesome, but it was cheap and not awful.

As they walked to the car, she wondered if Holden would call her. Now that he and Portia were no longer engaged, he had no reason not to call her.

This morning she'd been hurt, but she could understand. And she was sure he wasn't the kind of man who would use his penis like a burglar with a gun— shooting and running.

She'd expected to hear from him earlier, but maybe he was busy with something else....

———

Holden was on the patio, furiously painting when the call came. He didn't want to stop to answer, but the ring snapped him out of his creative frenzy as quickly as if someone had dropped a bucketful of ice onto his head. He studied his newest painting of Abby, wrapped in a cloud, only her shoulders, neck and face showing, her eyes slumberous, her smile satisfied.

The phone rang again, and he reluctantly set down the paintbrush and headed into the living room. He picked up his phone, and the display showed one name. *Juliana.*

His muscles tensed, he pressed Talk but couldn't say anything. If he did, it would be cutting and angry. The Juliana he knew would hang up on him, and that wouldn't be any help to Cara.

"Holden?" Juliana's voice sounded weak and thin. If not for her name on his display, he wouldn't have known it was her.

"I've been trying to reach you," he said, and his tone was gentle, though two seconds ago he'd been ready to verbally obliterate her.

"I know you have Cara. I'm sorry. I talked to my mother.

He took a seat on a chair that faced the sunset falling over the lake. "Did you tell her—"

"I can't." Her voice wavered. "Please don't make me tell her."

"Your parents ignore Cara. You're..." *A terrible mother.* But he clamped his lips together, unable to say it.

"Sick," she whispered. "I'm sick."

"Are you in a hospital?"

"Not that kind of sick. It's rehab."

"How long have you been there?"

"Six weeks. I'm at the halfway point."

"And then what?"

"I'm thinking of spending time at a meditation center in Arizona. I don't know how long. I can't go back to my parents."

"Neither can Cara. She's six now. When I first got her from your parents, she was afraid to talk. She's opening up now."

Sobs came from the other end of the phone.

He took a breath and went on. "It's not me who's helping her feel better, it's her caregiver. She raised her sister after their parents died. She has cats and a dog. Cara's already adopted a white kitten that Abby was fostering."

"She can't take the kitten to my mother's house. My father is allergic to pet hair."

"Your father rarely sees her."

"Yes, but kittens get loose. I tried to hide one in my room when I was Cara's age. I was very careful to keep the door shut all the time, but it snuck out anyway. My parents took it to the pound."

"There's a solution." He squared his shoulders though she wasn't there to see him. "She wants to stay with me."

"But she's not..." She sucked in a shaky breath then whispered, "Yours. She's not your child."

"She doesn't know that. She was forced on me by your parents, then they ran. They said two weeks, and I thought I could handle two weeks. And I have." He heard the surprise in his voice. "It's been going well."

Soft sobs came from the other side of the phone, and he kept talking. "She needed me. I couldn't throw her away. She thinks I'm her father. She feels secure here. I think she even feels...loved. Do you want to talk to her? She's sleeping now."

"No! I can't." Her thin voice rose, and he easily imagined her wringing her hands. "Don't you see I can't?"

"I see that, but can you see that you can't keep her in this limbo world? She needs a home where people care for her."

"I know, I know, I know." Her voice wobbled. "I'll think about it. This woman...the one you said helped her..."

"Abby."

"Yes! Abby, short for Abigail. Her name means maidservant, you know."

He smiled. Despite her way with pets and children—and men—Abby was no maidservant. "She's a wonderful woman."

Another moment of silence came from the other end of the phone. "Are you emotionally involved with this woman?"

"Yes."

"In love?"

Now it was his turn to pause. "I think so. It's too soon to commit to anything."

She laughed, full-throated with confidence and sensuality. This was one subject she was an expert at—

the relationships between men and women. "Look how fast you fell in love with me."

"I was captivated by you," he said.

"I know. You weren't my type, but you loved me so much."

Not love, he thought. Enthralled. She was so lively and ethereal...and needy. He'd wanted to cherish her forever. He'd wanted to make her whole.

"Is that how you feel about this woman?"

"No." Emotion rose in him, a rush of warmth in his chest. Abby was already whole, with so many facets to her it would take a lifetime to discover them all. And there was nothing ethereal about her. What he felt for her was solid and earthy. And it wasn't sex, though sex was part of it. It was...

"She's...everything," he said.

"Everything?" Her voice rose and ended with a quiver. "That sounds like love to me."

He scratched his eyebrow again then remembered the paint. "Let's get back to Cara. Legally, I'm her father. I'll take custody. When you're well, you can visit with her, and we'll see about shared custody."

"You would do this for me?"

"I would do this for Cara."

His words set off soft sobs from the other side of the phone. He closed his eyes for a second. He should be angry at her, but all he could do was pity her.

"What's your lawyer's name?" he asked, gazing at the horizon across Angel Lake, the deep pink bleeding into the gray. The way he thought the world sometimes bled.

Juliana's lawyer was the same one she'd had for their divorce, a sensible woman who'd been pleased they weren't going for each other's jugular. Juliana swore she'd call her, and he hoped she would.

They hung up, and he gathered his paints and his painting, taking them inside to clean the brushes and wash his hands. After that, he looked in on Cara. She was fast asleep. The kitten on her bed jumped to the floor and followed him into the living room. When he sat down, she leaped onto his lap, purring.

"I'm not good with kittens," he told her. But she didn't seem to understand as she purred and kneaded his legs. He sat back and fought an urge to pick up the phone and call Abby.

She was...perfectly imperfect. When he was with her, he wanted to smile. To kiss her. To laugh with her.

She seemed to be attracted to him. She even seemed to like him and feel romantic about him.

But when she knew him better, that might change.

The thought chilled him, as if there were ice in his veins.

And it was so soon. Love didn't happen this quickly. Only mistakes happened this fast and this fevered.

So he kept petting Epic until she stopped purring. By then it was too late to call Abby. It had taken all his willpower to hold back, and he went to bed with one thought on his mind.

Tomorrow. Tomorrow he would see Abby.

21

The humans were not behaving well.

"I'd like to talk to you," Holden said to Mom in the kitchen, with Cara looking on.

Even before Mom stiffened, Minnie knew he'd made a mistake with his harsh voice. He should pay attention to Quigley and her. When they wanted Mom's attention, they made their voices soft and melodic. Their way of saying, *Here I am. I'm allowing you to pet me now. I'll even rub my scent all over you so you'll know that I marked you as mine.*

And then they would dance on her legs, knead her, and purr. Let her know that her attentions made them happy.

But not Holden. He stood back, with his body as stiff as his voice. When Minnie had been a kitten all alone in the city, she'd run into a barbed wire fence that hurt her badly. It had made her cry and bleed.

Holden was a human wrapped inside an invisible barbed wire.

Mom gave Cara a stick with a string with feathers and told her to take it into the living room to play with Epic.

Unable to resist the feathers, Quigley rushed into the living room ahead of Epic. Cara looked back at Mom and Holden with a pucker in her forehead, then Quigley jumped up to grab the feathers and failed, and Epic followed his lead. Neither of them got anything, but they jumped again, and Cara laughed, her attention on the cats.

Minnie turned her back on them, ignoring the tug to run over and grab the feathers in her quick claws. That was play; this was important. Both Mom's and Holden's faces were almost mad. Their eyes blazed at each other, and tension snapped in the air like lightning bolts in a rumbling sky.

Holden stepped up to Abby. "Should we sit?"

Mom raised her eyebrows at Holden. "I can talk perfectly well standing up."

Minnie settled on the floor and wished there was a sunny spot in the room. If only they could understand her, she would tell them what to do:

First, be nice. Talk in beguiling tones. Rub your bodies against each other. That's important.

If it's not going the way you want, then talk loudly and long. Make them listen.

If that doesn't work, you should go into another room, dig your claws into the scratching pad—or whatever else is available. Continue until you tire yourself out, then you can take a drink of water and find a place to curl up and sleep.

Minnie didn't know what was wrong with the human brain; she just knew the world would be a better place if humans thought like cats.

———

Abby cleared the breakfast dishes off the table as Holden talked to her.

"I'm sorry," he said.

She kept her head down. Sorry for what? Getting sweaty with her in her bed?

Getting the best sex he'd ever had in his life?

Because she was good in bed. She knew it. Damn good.

"It's been such a short time since we'd met again," he continued. "Not even two weeks."

Her hand clenched around the handle of a fork. She forced her grip to relax then carried the dishes to the counter. He just realized the number of days passing now and not two nights ago?

Jerk.

She set the dishes on the counter and wanted to kick him again.

"I want you to understand. I'd like to explore this thing between us. See where it's going." His voice was stiff. "I don't think either of us want to make rash decisions."

She clenched her teeth so tightly her gums hurt. Understand? Of course she understood. He was a rat bastard, and she wanted to kick him multiple times. In one specific area.

Explore "this thing between them"? She knew what that "thing" was, and he wasn't getting it anywhere near her. Not after this.

"Will you say something?"

She finished wiping the table and straightened and finally looked at him.

The closed-teeth smile she gave him made him jerk back, a sign that he wasn't completely dense.

"No problem," she said. "I understand perfectly. I heard from Sam that your engagement is off, and you don't want me to get the wrong idea. Don't worry. I now have the right idea about you. You'd better leave. I'm sure you have very important things to do at work."

"This is important, too."

She shrugged. "Not anymore."

He held his hands out to her. "Abby—"

"Stop right there." Gripping the dishrag, she stepped back. "You come any closer, and you're going to be sorry."

"I didn't handle this right."

"Now I need *handling*?" She pointed to the door and lowered her voice. "Just go. Right now. Just go."

"That's not what I..." He stared at her for seconds, then his lips flattened together in the frustrated way men did when they realized there were no words to describe their idiocy—yet they still wouldn't admit it to themselves or anyone else—and he looked at her for ten seconds like that, giving her a chance to change her mind. Finally, he nodded curtly, called goodbye to Cara, then left.

The screen door clanked shut, and a soft cry came from behind Abby. She spun around and saw Cara standing in the kitchen, the outer corners of her mouth and her eyes curved down, sadness bleeding out of her pores.

Oh shit.

"Are you mad at Daddy?"

Abby stepped toward her. "Honey, I'm not happy with him, but it's nothing to do with you. I...love you."

"You do?" The downturned eye and mouth corners smoothed away. "You do love me?" Her voice squeaked.

"Yes, I do." With a little laugh that sounded almost like a sob, Abby crouched, her arms out.

Cara ran to her and slammed into her chest, grabbing Abby around her neck. Abby held on to Cara to keep from tumbling onto her butt. Then she got her balance and, with an oomph, stood. Holding Cara tightly, she twirled her around as giggles spilled from Cara's mouth, and laughter spilled from hers.

When she stopped, they still laughed breathlessly, and it took a minute before the room stopped turning. Only then did she see the two cats, one kitten, and the dog sitting at the juncture where the living room turned into the kitchen, watching them.

It seemed to Abby that their gazes were approving, as if they were thinking, *At last she's doing something right.*

Over their heads, she saw a navy blue car drive away from the curb.

Screw you, she thought, her mouth tensing. Screw you.

Apparently she was a bad judge of men. Before, she hadn't cared about her bad choices. She'd picked men for a fun time, nothing more. Holden had been different. At least, that's what her deluded brain had told her.

Yeah, right. How often had she heard other women say that?

She wished she had kicked him.

Then Cara kissed her cheek, and her heart clenched, and her eyes prickled. "Ooh," Abby said, and held Cara to her chest, Cara's legs gangling against her thighs.

"I love you back," Cara said. "I wish you were my mommy."

Tears sprang into Abby's eyes. This was the fourth time Cara had wished that. And for the third time, she whispered, "I wish I were, too."

But that was never, ever going to happen.

———

An hour and a half after Holden left, a small truck with Eagleton Furniture painted in big letters on the side was parked in front of Abby's house, and a young man of average appearance handed her a large, padded envelope. He gave her a long, searching look and admired Lion. She signed the receipt then closed the door.

"What's that?" Cara had disappeared into Grace's bedroom until the delivery man left, and Abby wondered if she was afraid someone was coming to take her away.

Abby headed for the table. "I don't know. I think it's from your dad."

"Really?" Cara ran to the table to see.

The envelope felt thick and stiff, with tape across the envelope flap. Abby fetched a steak knife to carefully slice open the top. As she pulled the contents out, she saw it was an unframed canvas, about eighteen by twenty-four. The background was a gauzy green, and in the middle of it was a floating image of—

She gasped, and Cara squeaked.

"That's you!" she said with a squeal. "That's you, Abby."

"Yes, it is." She felt dazed. More dazed now than after she'd twirled Cara. It was her yet not her. She looked like...a fairy-tale version of herself, her expression dreamy and yet...sensual.

She shivered.

"Did my daddy paint this?"

Abby lowered her gaze to the right corner and saw the name *Holden Ramsay* scrawled in black; below it was the month and year.

"Apparently he did."

When she'd pulled out the canvas, a paper had slid halfway out. She set the painting down to read the paper.

"What does it say?" Cara asked, on the tips of her toes as she tried to read the words on the paper: *The first painting I did of you.*

Abby's heart thumped. She looked back to the painting and noticed she was wearing the turquoise shorts and the lime-green top that Abby was pretty sure she'd worn the first time he'd picked up Cara. Nothing like being colorful.

"He said thank you," she said, her gaze going back to the painting, wondering if that was how he saw her.

"For what?"

Abby looked at her. "For being so amazing."

Cara pealed with laughter as Abby stared back down on it.

What did this mean? This painting of her was so...beautiful. Was that how he saw her?

And why had he painted it? What was he trying to tell her? Was this his idea of an apology?

"Are you still mad at my daddy?"

"I wasn't mad at him."

Cara knitted her forehead, and Abby felt a tug on her heart. The way she felt when she welcomed a nervous new cat into her home. One that might have been neglected or abused and was watching her to see what she might do. Searching her face and her gestures and her voice. Attuned to changes in her emotions, because she was the one they depended on and they'd been disappointed before, over and over again, and were afraid to trust. Afraid to believe.

"Okay," she said, looking down at Cara's sad, upturned face, "maybe I was mad at him, but that's nothing to do with the way I feel about you. Didn't I tell you I love you?"

Cara's face scrunched, and she surged forward and threw her arms around Abby's waist, hanging on tightly, her face pressed against Abby's belly. Bending over the girl, Abby put her hands on Cara's back. For the second time that day, tears burned her eyes.

They stayed that way for a very long time.

22

When Holden picked up Cara, he didn't mention the painting. Neither did Abby, though it felt as if it were a live thing waiting for her in the top drawer of her desk. Hidden from her eyes but not her mind. And certainly not her emotions that were as mixed up as if they'd been stuffed in a super blender for twenty minutes.

The next day, she got another padded envelope handed to her by the same average-looking young man with the interesting name of Ogden, according to the name on his pocket. Ogden called her "ma'am." She stifled a groan and told him to call her Abby.

She thanked Ogden and closed the door as Cara squealed and clapped her hands. "Is that from Daddy?"

"I think so." She opened it, and inside was a second painting of her floating in a whitish, sunshine-shot background. This was mostly her face, though she recognized the grass-green top she'd been wearing. On that day, she was laughing. She looked...almost unreal. Like a happy angel instead of a woman. He'd gotten that wrong. She could be critical of other people. She could be messy. She could be unforgiving. He must not have seen that side of her.

She had faults. Lots of faults.

"That's you!" Cara danced around the living room. "That's you!"

Feeling unaccountably light, Abby danced with her.

After they danced, she found the note that said, *The second painting I did of you.*

She stared at the words for a long time, as if she could decipher a hidden meaning. But she could no more understand it than she understood what was going on in his head.

When he picked up Cara, she thanked him for the painting again. He looked at her as if expecting something more, but she still harbored a desire to kick him.

Only this time, after kicking him, she wanted to kiss him.

Instead of doing either, she hugged Cara goodbye then watched them walk away.

On Wednesday, Ogden came to her door again. By this time, they were using first names, and even Cara said, "Hi, Ogden!" In this painting, she looked sad and vulnerable. She wondered what she'd been thinking of. How much she still missed her mom and dad, though they'd been gone for nine years? The problems with the barn? The fact that she had raised her sister, but she was twenty-eight and didn't have a child of her own? That she hadn't had a boyfriend in two years?

The note said it was the third painting he'd done of her. She frowned at it. Maybe another woman might feel flattered, but by this time, she wished he'd *talk* to her instead of writing the stupid notes.

On Thursday, she received the fourth painting—and right after it, a phone call from a man with a deep voice who said he was Simon Finbar.

"My angel!" she said.

With a rumbling laugh, he said his ex-wife would argue that he was closer to the devil.

The laugh brought back an image from the meeting in Oshkosh with the five members of the investment group as they'd asked her questions. She remembered him now: a thin man about five nine, in his fifties with short gray hair, his face scored with deep smile lines. Definitely a man with a little of the devil in him.

But she didn't care about his ancestry. She only cared about his money.

She asked about his mother, though. He said she was as fine as she could be and was staying with him for a while. Her and her cats, and she was interested in seeing the cat furniture, too. Today.

Holding back a squeal, she arranged to meet him and his mother at the barn in an hour.

When she hung up, she let out her squeal then lifted Cara in her arms and twirled her around, both of them laughing. Setting Cara down, she told her about the angel who was really a man with money. Then she called Sam, who didn't answer but was probably working with something that drowned out the phone's ring. Grace was at school taking an advanced English class, and Abby texted her about the angel investor, adding that she'd better not be reading it until the class was over.

After that, she kissed Minnie, Quigley, Lion, and Epic, who had been awakened from their various naps, first by Ogden and then by Simon's call. The pets gathered around them, watching them intently, as if taking in every word they said and every nuance in their facial expressions.

Cara kissed them all, too, and told Epic they'd be back soon. Two minutes later, they were driving to the outskirts of Eagleton, straight toward Abby's bright and shining future.

———

When Holden picked up Cara, he saw the change in Abby. She had a bounce in her step, and she looked like she wanted to break into a dance. But she just thanked him for the picture, hugged Cara, and stood in the doorway to wave them goodbye.

At his house, Cara set the table for the takeout he'd picked up on the drive home. He spooned out half the sweet and sour shrimp for her, while he piled Mongolian pork on a plate for him. They both dug in. So far, he'd held himself from pumping Cara for information, but if she didn't tell him soon...

She was about one-eighth through the sweet and sour shrimp when he asked how her day was.

"Lots happened today," Cara said.

"What's that?" he asked. "Did Abby say anything about the painting?"

"Uh-uh. Right after Ogden left, Abby got a call from an angel." Her voice rose, and she peered at him with an expectant smile.

"An angel? I didn't know they used phones."

Cara giggled. "Not a real angel. He's really a man with money."

Holden set down his fork. "Is that what she said?"

Cara nodded vigorously. "She didn't want me to feel bad when I saw he didn't have wings. But I already knew he couldn't be a real angel."

"Why?"

"Because real angels are ladies." She stared at him, the expression on her face telling him that she couldn't believe he didn't know this. "And they have wands, too."

"That's good to know. In case I ever come across one."

She frowned. Clearly doubting that an angel would ever come to him. He suspected she was right.

"He came to see the furniture. His mom came with him. She was old." Her eyebrows rose. "Really old. She used a walker to help her walk."

"What did the angel decide?"

"I don't know, but Abby wants him to invest in her business. Then they can make the cat furniture in a nicer place, and they can pay someone to help Sam. Wouldn't that be nice?"

He nodded glumly. Abby deserved to catch a break.

"Abby was happy on the drive home. She laughed a lot."

"That's nice." He looked down at his Mongolian pork and decided he was never going to order it again.

"Daddy?"

He looked up at her and saw her forehead was puckered, and he knew she was going to ask a question he wouldn't want to answer.

"You have money. Why don't you be Abby's angel?"

"It's not as simple as that."

"Why not? You can even have her work in your place. I heard you and Uncle Ryan saying there was an empty building. Why not let Sam work there?"

"It's complicated."

She pushed her plate away. "I'm not hungry anymore."

"Don't you want dessert? I have ice cream."

She looked at him for a long moment then shrugged. "Okay," she said, as if she was doing him a favor by eating ice cream.

"Has she said anything about my paintings?" he asked as he got to his feet.

She sighed. "If you want to know what she thinks, Daddy, you should just ask her."

His movements slow, he gathered their plates and silverware. Cara didn't understand that asking questions was even more complicated. And as for investing in Abby's business, that would multiply the complications.

But if he didn't...

He might be making the biggest mistake of his life.

———

When the phone rang, Abby was celebrating with mint chocolate chip ice cream. But she jumped up and left it on the table. Grace was at a friend's house and would be home later tonight, and she wanted to talk to someone who would share her happiness. Her lips already forming a smile, she looked at the phone and saw Holden's name.

She froze and stared at it as it rang again then three more times. She stood there, unable to pick it up.

This man had made love to her. Wonderful, amazing love. More than that, he'd made her feel cherished. Cared for. It had been so long since someone had made her feel like that. Much too long.

And then he'd turned cold on her. He'd run scared.

And now he was sending her the paintings every day....

And they were so...amazing. As if he'd infused love into every brushstroke.

Yet he'd walked away from her. Acted as if she were just a babysitter and he her employer.

She couldn't handle that, and she didn't need to handle it.

The voice mail clicked on, and her body jerked. At her sides, she curled her hands into fists.

"Abby," he said, "this is Holden."

A choked laugh came out of her mouth. He was so formal. So...proper. How insane was it that she found it sexy?

"Cara told me about your angel. I just called to congratulate you. If you need any business advice, I'll be happy to help you." There was a pause. "Call me," he said, his voice a hoarse whisper. Then he hung up; her voice mail stopped.

Her shoulders slumped, and she closed her eyes so tight she felt dizzy. A noise made her open her eyes and look down into a pair of Siamese-blue eyes. She scooped up Minnie, who draped herself against her, as if she knew that a hot rush of loneliness smoldered inside her. Knew that a longing clawed at her heart.

With Minnie marking her jaw, she headed into the living room and sank onto the couch. Quigley hopped up on one side, and Lion hopped on the other. He wasn't supposed to sit on the couch, but she knew he did when she was gone. She'd seen the evidence in his short, golden hairs on the green couch, often accompanied by bits of leaves and grass and sometimes pieces of dried mud.

Right now, she didn't care. Right now was the right time to break that stupid rule. Right now, he was putting his head on her thigh and making a sad noise in his throat, empathizing with her.

Quigley was rubbing his head on the other side of her jaw. She petted both cats then managed to pet Lion while still holding Minnie.

"I love you," she said. "Why do I need a man when I have all of you?"

Minnie immediately started meowing in various tones and syllables, staring into her eyes, obviously saying something important. Quigley joined in, louder, but saying less than Minnie. He'd always been more of a doer than a talker.

Only Lion looked at her with those sad, brown eyes and didn't need to say anything more.

She petted them for a long time before she remembered her ice cream. She let go of Minnie and headed back to the kitchen. By that time it had melted, but she ate it anyway. When she was done, she set it on the floor and let Lion lick out the bowl. It gave her a sense of satisfaction to realize that if Holden were there, he would disapprove. He might even be horrified.

Good thing she didn't have to worry about the way he felt about anything.

23

Holden stood inside Abby's kitchen. It was messy this morning, with her laptop and the newspaper on the table. So was her checkbook, and he guessed that was the reason for the frown on her forehead.

"We need to talk," she said as Cara ran into Grace's bedroom to play a game on the computer with cats and dogs.

Holden breathed easier, relieved that Abby brought it up. "About your business, yes."

"No, about Cara. She's staying with you now, right? Our arrangement was for two weeks. Have you found a place for her next week?"

"This arrangement seemed to be working so well. I thought—"

"You may have thought a lot of things, but you haven't told me any of it."

He rubbed the back of his head. "Can you take care of her?"

She stared at him, her mouth rebellious, which wasn't a good sign. "We're getting an investor. I'll be busy finding a new place to make the furniture. I'll need to hire people. An IT person. A marketer. A—"

"Don't."

"What?"

"Don't go with him." He spoke with his voice low so Cara wouldn't hear him in Grace's bedroom...and so

Abby wouldn't hear the torture in his voice. "I talked to Portia last night."

She raised her eyebrows, clearly not impressed.

"Sam had told her that your angel is Simon Finbar," he went on, feeling like a clumsy elephant about to be jumped on by a sleek lion. "I know Simon. He's a womanizer."

"A what?"

"You know. A horndog."

Her eyebrows went up, but she didn't say anything.

"Ask Portia. She'll tell you he put the moves on her, too."

She crossed her arms. "Apparently Portia and I have had the same experience with more than one man."

He grimaced. "I deserve that."

"I've had men make passes at me before, and I know how to say no." Her eyes narrowed. "If I want to."

"Abby—"

"Stop." She held up her hand. "You don't get to warn me about other men. Not after what happened last week."

"I didn't handle it well."

"Whatever you're thinking of saying, don't. In the first place, I don't have to be *handled*. In the second place—"

"I was stupid. We were going too fast, and I just wanted to take it slower. But I didn't want to stop it."

"You don't seem to know what you want. I can't handle your indecision. I want a man who knows what he wants."

"I do know. I want *you*."

"That's what you're saying now, but how do I know what you'll say tomorrow?"

"I've been saying it all week."

"That's funny. I didn't hear you say anything."

"I didn't say it." He heard the torture in his voice. "I *showed* you how I felt. With the paintings."

She put her hand over her mouth. Instead of looking pleased, she looked stunned, as if he'd socked her in her belly.

He put his hand on the side of her face, stroking his thumb over her cheekbone. "Give me another chance."

She stepped back from him, crossing her arms again. "You're right. It was too fast. Maybe we can...see each other again. But not now. Now I have to..." She sucked in her lips and looked away. "Concentrate on my business. This is something I've been working for, hoping for. And maybe Simon's not the ideal person to go with."

"Because he's a horndog," he said.

Her laugh sounded choked. "I told you I can handle that. It's because of the terms he wants. It's more than Sam and I wanted to give a backer. Sam and I will talk about it again today, but I don't think we can say no. We might never get this chance again."

"Yes, you can. With me."

"What?" Her eyes widened.

"We have an empty building." He laughed and gestured toward the office. "We could rent you the space and equipment."

"We can't afford it."

"I can afford it."

She took another step back. "I don't think it's a good idea."

"I'm not proposing this out of lust for you. I've seen your work. I believe in your business. And I know your passion. Ryan does, too. He's the one who originally thought of this."

"Really? When was this?"

"Last week."

"And you're first mentioning this to me now?" She crossed her arms again.

"I should just take off my shoe," he said, wincing, "and shove it in my mouth and keep it there."

"Sounds good to me."

He raked his hand through his hair. "When Ryan said it, I knew how I felt about you already. I was engaged, and if I was around you all the time, I knew I wouldn't be able to..." He stopped, watching her face freeze more with every syllable. "Nothing I can say will make this better, will it?"

"No."

"I didn't pull back because I wasn't sure about my feelings. I was unsure about yours."

"Then you should ask me."

"Maybe now, but you don't know me." His throat closed up, but he swallowed, opening it. If he wanted to move forward—and he did—there were things that needed to be said. "No one has loved me in my life. Not my parents, not my grandparents, not my first wife, not Portia."

Her lips parted, her face stricken. "None of that's *your* fault."

He wanted to touch her but held back. "I thought maybe we could do this slowly—"

She gave a laugh that held tears. "Too late for that."

Once again, his throat closed, and he swallowed again. "I'm not sorry."

"Me neither."

"I don't want to lose you. I have to say it now. I'm crazy about you."

"Or just crazy," she said.

She was breaking his heart, but he wanted to laugh. "I've been too sane for too many years," he said. "Maybe it's time I went a little crazy."

Her eyes moistened again. "And I've been too crazy for too many years, and maybe it's time I started to think like you do. Maybe we should take it slow. And I don't know if I should mix business and pleasure."

"You haven't seen what I could offer you."

Her gaze flicked down then up. "Oh, I thought I'd seen everything you had to offer."

Cara's laughter came from down the hall. He peered over Abby's head, and as Abby turned, too, Grace's laughter joined Cara's, but neither showed in the hall. When Abby turned back to him, he could see the softening in her mouth and eyes. He felt the same melting feeling inside him.

"Cara," he said. "I can offer you Cara."

She sucked in a breath, and her face scrunched. "You don't play fair. Let's just keep this about business. Don't make it personal. Not now."

The knotted muscles in his shoulders loosened. *Not now* meant *later*. It meant *possibilities*. That's all he needed right now. All he could hope for.

"Okay, let's keep it to business. Eagleton Furniture would be a good fit with your company. Though our products are aimed at different end users, think of the promo possibilities. A 'buy US furniture' campaign isn't news, but 'buy US cat and people furniture' is. That combo would make the news. That would be something that people would talk about. The publicity alone will make it a gold mine."

A line creased her forehead. "I don't know... You could be right."

He opened his mouth then shut it. He needed to let her work it out herself.

"It would be something that even the talk shows would mention," she said slowly. "We could make videos showing the cat furniture with cat customers next to the people furniture with people sitting on them."

As she talked, he pictured it in his mind.

Her head cocked slightly downward, her eyebrows contracting as she said, "Send me an email with everything you're offering and what you want in return. I'll forward it to Sam. I told Simon we'd tell him yes or no by Monday. I'll tell you by Monday, too."

Another peal of Cara's laughter came from Grace's room. Abby closed her eyes tight. Seconds later she opened them, and her gaze burned into his. "Bring Cara with you on Monday. I'll work out something with Grace and pay her for the hours she spends with Cara. When Cara's more secure and confident, you can find a good daycare facility. She told Grace that she's her first friend. She needs to interact with children her own age."

Emotion filled him, hopefulness mixed with sadness that people who had no family relationship with Cara were the ones who were concerned about making her happy. "You're pretty wonderful."

"I'm *fabulous*." She laughed a little wildly. "I've been fostering kittens for three years. A child deserves the same care as a cat."

"What about me?" he asked. "What do I deserve?"

"From me?" She raised her eyebrows. "An answer on Monday. I think you should leave now. Your boss won't like it if you're late to work."

He laughed harshly, turned, and left.

———

With Cara in the house, Minnie's naps were disturbed more often during the day than before she'd come into their lives. First she'd been like a small mouse who squeaked once in a while, as if afraid to make too much noise. But now she was noisier, like a regular human child.

If Minnie really wanted to, she could find a perch to nap on, a place where no one could find her. But the days were more interesting with Cara in the house. There was more laughter and noise and less quiet. Minnie didn't always like noise, but she liked happy noises.

Today Cara and Grace were chattering. Only Mom was quiet, but no one seemed to notice except Minnie.

And no one seemed to notice the strain in Mom's voice when Cara's dad came to the house just before it was time for the humans to eat. Not even Quigley and Lion.

They only noticed the way he looked at Mom, as if she were a piece of tuna and he wanted to snap her up before any other man got a whiff of her.

They only noticed the mating smell.

Humans weren't much different from cats and dogs, Minnie thought.

When Mom hugged Cara goodbye, she smelled of sadness.

After much reflection, Minnie came to a decision. There were two ways Mom could go—the wrong way or the right way.

Minnie would have to make sure she would go the right way.

If Minnie saw a kitten teetering on the top of a perch, hesitating over jumping down, Minnie would give the kitten a push. Not out of meanness to see her tumble down to the floor—though that was always amusing—but jumping down was what cats were meant to do. It was the right thing to do.

And if she didn't push Mom off the perch, she might end up doing the wrong thing.

But Minnie couldn't do it alone.

She tackled Quigley first. Of course, he said yes, eager to prove his prowess.

Lion was next. They needed Lion. Though Minnie didn't like to admit it, Lion had a better sense of smell than she had. Of course, her hearing and brainpower were superior. But for this adventure, she needed Lion.

She told him if they didn't do it, Mom would get hurt.

Lion didn't ask why; he just said yes.

Dogs were so easy.

Now all they needed to do was to watch for a chance to escape....

24

Mom screamed at them to come back. The screen door hadn't quite closed when she'd gone outside to dig in the patch of dirt she called a garden. Mom wasn't as vigilant about making sure the door caught now that Quigley and Lion were older. Minnie had no desire to go outside. Outside had bad things—dogs that wanted to eat her, cars that wanted to run her over, and people who wanted to hurt her. It had no water, no food, no people to pet her and tell her how wonderful she was.

Indoors had everything good—soft places to curl up on, warmth in winter, coolness in summer, food and water, hugs and kisses.

Unlike her, Quigley had always been an indoor cat, and he didn't know what it was like to go outside.

Lion would go outdoors, but he did whatever Mom said, even when he didn't wear the leash.

Not now, though. Now they ran, their hearts thumping too fast. With her superior hearing, Minnie could hear the pounding of all three hearts, hear their fast breaths and their paws hitting the grass and then the click of their nails against the hardness of the sidewalk and a duller click when they ran onto the street.

And she could hear Mom's shouts, hear her fear and her desperation.

Brakes squealed, a horn hooted, the sounds hurting Minnie's ears. They reached the other side of the street, and Mom's cries to them grew more frantic. Quigley was at Lion's side, and Minnie was just behind them. Quigley and she could easily outrun Lion, but they needed him to guide them with his nose.

Right now, Minnie could smell the remnants of fumes from Holden's car, but she knew the trail was stronger to Lion's nose.

Finally they were far enough away from home to hear Mom's calls only faintly. They still ran, but not as fast, when a growl stopped them. Two dogs stood on the sidewalk, facing them. They both had the widest jaws Minnie had ever seen and the biggest teeth. And the way the dogs faced them, with meanness in their eyes, it looked as if they wanted to use their big teeth to bite them.

She, Quigley, and Lion stopped.

The two dogs snarled.

Dinner, the dog nearest the grass said with a growl.

Dessert, the dog nearest the road said with a louder growl.

Minnie's claws extracted. She didn't look at Quigley but knew his did, too.

Get out of our way, Quigley said.

Lion looked at the dogs. *You heard the cat.*

The dogs growled more deeply, their muscles bunching, their bodies preparing to attack.

Minnie jumped, landing on the back of the dog nearest the street. In the time it took him to yowl, she'd reached down and clawed his muzzle, missing his eye by a hair.

He yipped in pain and shook her off. The other dog, a female, yipped, too, as Quigley copied her moves. Minnie was about to jump on the dog's back again when Lion bit his flank then turned to the other.

But the other dog was already running away from them, blood dripping from her claw-torn ear.

Their breaths harsh, they watched the dogs disappear behind the back of a house. Then they ran along the sidewalk again, away from the smell of fresh blood.

Did you see me? Quigley asked. *I'm a warrior.*

We're all warriors, Minnie said, picturing the bleeding muzzle of the male dog.

Her heart was beating even faster than before. The scent of blood was still on her claws, and she felt...alive. All her senses working at their highest level.

They hadn't run long when Lion slowed at a corner. Minnie had lost the exhaust smell blocks ago, and alarm knifed through her. *Did you—* she began, when Lion interrupted her.

The car turned here. He ran in the opposite direction of the center of the city.

As the blocks went by, their pace slowed, and Lion panted. They never stopped, though, still in a half run.

There's water ahead, Lion said, speeding up again.

Minnie smelled the water as they reached the next block. She remembered the smell from when she was little. Its scent was different from the water Mom gave her. It smelled like earth and leaves as well as water.

As they reached a house much bigger than Mom's, Lion slowed, panting harder now, his body heaving. There was a leafy tree on the side of the house not far from her.

He's here, Lion said. *So are Cara and Epic.*

He didn't have to tell Minnie that. She smelled them already.

Lion plopped down in the shade of the tree. Quigley followed the smell of water. Minnie couldn't see the water, but she could smell that it was close. Instead of following him, she rubbed her mouth against Lion's face, her way of thanking him.

Only then did she go to the back of the house where the land sloped downward. She half-slid, half-dashed down it then stepped delicately into the water with the bugs and the little pieces of dirt, twigs, and leaves. Quigley was already drinking, and she lowered her head and lapped the cold water.

She was still lapping when Lion joined her and Quigley. He stepped deeper into the lake, splashing her and Quigley as he passed them. They protested, but not too loudly. After all, he'd led them here.

After they drank their fill, they collapsed on the grassy edge. It felt safe here. No cars, no people, no other animals except the birds—and they kept their distance from the three of them. Minnie's stomach was still full. Knowing she was leaving the house, she'd eaten more of her dry food than usual, as had Quigley.

Of course, cats were hunters, and they could find their own food. But she remembered when she was on her own. She'd been too young to be a hunter. Instead, other animals had hunted her, and she'd had to hide from them, squeezing into places too small for them to find. She'd been starving when Mom had found her and taken her in and cried over her and said, "I'm your mom now."

And she'd been Minnie's mom ever since then. Feeding her, petting her, loving her. She had soft hands, a soft voice, and soft kisses. Since Minnie's cat mom had gone away without her, life had been hard. But then she'd found Mom, and softness had come back into her life.

That was a long time ago, but Minnie never forgot.

Mom had helped her; maybe she had saved her. Now it was time for Minnie to do something back for Mom.

After she napped.

But not here, in the open.

We need to go by the house.

Lion, who had his eyes closed, opened them. *In the house? With Cara?*

Not now. In the morning.

Lion lifted his head from the grass. *Sleep outside?*

It's not cold out. It's not raining. You've taken naps in the backyard before.

In the daytime. When the sun is out. I'm not like you. I sleep during the night.

Good. Then you won't even know you'll be in the open. Because you'll be sleeping all night.

And I'll watch for big animals that want to eat you, Quigley said. *I'm strong and brave and fast.*

And stupid, Minnie thought, standing.

But I still don't understand, Lion said, not getting up. In general, he was easygoing, but sometimes he got stubborn. *Why can't we go inside the house and sleep? Why do we have to stay outside?*

To make Mom worry.

I don't want to worry Mom.

When Mom worries, Quigley said, *she gets sad. I don't want Mom to be sad, either.*

Minnie flicked her ear at him. *The longer Mom worries, the happier she'll be when she finds us. Worry about us will make her remember what's important in her life.*

I'm important, Quigley said.

We're all important, Minnie said. *Mom loves us, and she loves Cara, and she wants to mate with Holden. She'll be so happy that we're safe with him that she'll kiss him and everything will be all right.*

And she'll see his big house, Quigley said, *and want to live with him.*

Minnie wasn't sure about that. She liked their smaller house just fine. But Quigley liked bigger things, and she needed him to be on her side, so she purred an agreement. Lion got up, and all three trotted to the back of the house. They settled in a spot where the building was behind them, and the patio was on one side. Protected by the house on two sides, they only had to watch for predators on the other two sides.

In the grass around them, the crickets sang, and the sun had started its downward journey. From inside the house, Minnie heard Cara's high voice and Holden's deeper rumble.

A meow came at the back door that was open on the inside. "Epic," Cara said, her voice floating out, "you can't go outside. Bad kitty."

Epic still meowed. Minnie didn't say anything, and neither did the others. Then the inside door closed.

Epic heard us, Lion said.

A phone rang, and they leaned closer to the house to hear better.

After saying hello, Holden let the person on the invisible side do the talking. Minnie's heart beat faster. The voice was small, but she heard enough to know it was Mom.

Holden didn't talk much. Mom was doing all the talking. Her voice wasn't loud enough for Minnie to understand the words, but the words tumbled out too fast and the pitch was high and trembly.

"Do you want me to look for them?" Holden asked.

A sob came from the other end of the phone. Minnie's head jerked up. Mom. She was crying!

Quigley made a sad sound, and Minnie ignored him. They were doing this for Mom's good. It had to work. The sadder Mom was now, the happier she would be when they were found.

"You're sure?" Holden said.

Mom said something, and Holden said, "Call us if...*when*...they come back."

Mom said something else, and Holden said, "Remember, if you need me, let me know and I'll be there."

Minnie concentrated hard but couldn't hear Mom's reply. Then Holden hung up, the call done.

Quigley was already telling Lion what he'd heard. Minnie lay down again and closed her eyes.

Sometimes humans needed to be scared.

Humans thought too much. Even Mom. When she was scared, she would stop thinking with her mind and think with her heart.

Minnie closed her eyes. No more talking. No more thinking. Her body wanted to sleep.

What if it doesn't work? Lion asked.

She kept her eyes closed and her mouth shut because she didn't have an answer.

Tomorrow morning they would see.

———

Abby walked along the streets, the sky a dark gray. Her feet were sore from covering blocks and blocks of the city sidewalks. And her throat was sore from calling the names of her pets.

No, not pets. Family.

It felt like it was happening to her again. Losing multiple members of her family at once.

Grief and fear welled up inside her chest and throat, choking her, strangling her heart.

A dog barked, and she turned her head. "Lion!" she called, her voice hoarse. "Lion."

The dog barked again, and this time she could tell the bark wasn't as full as Lion's. She put her hand over her mouth to hold back a sob then continued to trudge home.

Earlier, she'd insisted that Grace go to her friend's for another overnighter, telling Grace that she was sure the animals would come back soon. She'd even managed to dredge up a smile.

That's how she'd lived most of her life for the past nine years. Doing what she needed to do and keeping her smile on. Not letting anyone know how scared she was most of the time.

Not even herself. Not until today.

But before today, she'd had her cat, and then Lion, and then Quigley. She'd had their warm bodies, and she'd had their love.

She'd *thought* she had their love. She'd been as sure of it as she was sure there was a sky above her head and the earth beneath the soles of her sneakers.

Why had they left like that? Why had they run away from her? Minnie and Quigley only left the house to go to the vet, and she had to force them into the carriers.

"Are you okay?" a woman called.

She looked to the side and saw a man and a woman, probably not much older than her, sitting on the front porch, their light on. There was a tricycle on the sidewalk and a bicycle with training wheels.

They were normal people. Not like her. People thought she was normal, but that was because she pretended so well.

"I'm fine," she said, and her voice broke like a bad cell phone connection. She speeded up her pace, not wanting them to be nice to her. Not wanting the couple to pity her. She might start crying again.

She needed to go home. Maybe Minnie, Lion, and Quigley would be waiting for her.

She walked faster, though from the pain on the bottom of her right foot, she was pretty sure she was getting a blister. She was only five and a half blocks away from her small home, time enough for her thoughts to dwell on all the things she'd done wrong. The ways she'd failed Grace and failed her parents' memory. When they'd lived, she'd been one of those kids who thought her parents would always be there to pick her up if she fell. She'd taken advantage of it, and she'd run a little too wild for a while.

Then they'd died, and the money wasn't there, and she'd done the best she could, but her best was pretty crappy.

And now she finally had a chance to start her own business in a bigger way, but it was being offered at a high price.

Holden had made her another offer. Financially it might be better... But personally, the price could be her heart. And she didn't think she could afford that.

She couldn't even afford the loss of her two cats and one dog.

With them gone, none of the other stuff seemed to matter. Some people would say she was silly, that they were just pets. But to her, they were much more than that. They were family. The children she had never had. Somehow, she must have failed them.

She started to run, calling their names in a croaking voice until it cracked and the pain in her foot forced her to slow. Half-running with a limp, breathing harshly, she told herself that when she got home, they would be there, they would be there, they would be there...

Tears ran down her cheeks, and she scrubbed them off.

If she didn't find them soon, she didn't know what she would do.

25

A dog barking loudly snapped Holden out of a dream where he was running down the street searching for something and couldn't remember what that something was.

Then he heard a cat meow, but it sounded louder and fuller than Epic. And it seemed to come from his backyard, outside his bedroom.

He opened his eyes. The sun crept into his bedroom through the spaces around the drapes his designer had put up. Another meow came, this one thinner, coming from inside the house. Epic, his waking brain said.

Then two cats meowed outside the house.

The synapses in his brain started firing. *Abby's phone call. The two runaway cats. The runaway dog.*

He rolled out of bed and grabbed his pants from the chair near the window. He'd just zipped them up when his door banged open. Cara poked her head in the room, her eyes wide, her smile brilliant.

"Lion and Minnie and Quigley are outside! I can't open the door. I didn't see Abby. Is she here, too? Hurry, Daddy, hurry."

Before he could answer, she twirled and raced away, her bouncing blond hair, pink top, and blue shorts disappearing, her bare feet slapping on the wooden floor. He grabbed a shirt and pulled it on as he chased after her.

She reached the French doors before him, and was struggling to unlock them when he came up behind her.

"It's them, Daddy, it's them!" Cara danced away from the door handle. "Open the door! Open it!"

"I'm opening it." He pulled it open, and the cats darted into his house, the dog panting after them.

"Where's Abby? How come Abby's not with them?" Cara ran outside, yelling, "Abby! Abby! Where are you?"

"Cara, come back in." He followed her onto the patio in his bare feet. "She's not here. We have to call her."

Her forehead puckered, Cara turned back. "How do you know she's not here?"

He shoved his hand through his hair. "She called me last night and said the cats and dog were missing."

Her head tilted. "Why didn't you tell me?"

"I didn't want to worry you."

She looked at him for what seemed a long time but must have been only about ten seconds. "Next time tell me."

"I will," he said, even as he thought he wouldn't.

Adults were supposed to shield children.

She hurried past him. "Let's call her now."

Inside again, he picked up the phone and clicked on her number. Cara held out her hands. "Let me tell her, Daddy! Let me tell her."

He handed it to her, and just as she grabbed it, he heard Abby's voice say, "Holden? They still aren't—"

Cara whipped the phone to her ear. "It's me! Guess what? They're here!"

———

Abby pulled up the driveway to the Frank Lloyd Wright-style house that looked expensive and beautiful. Holden had said he would bring the three furry members of their family to their place, but she'd yelled the news to Grace, who'd come home from her sleepover early, too worried to laugh with her friends as if nothing had happened. Then Abby had grabbed her purse and car keys and said, "We're coming," and hung up.

Once in the SUV, she'd realized she didn't know his address, and she made Grace call to get it. Here they were now. Stopping the car. Getting out. Running to the front door. Heart beating too fast. Emotions too exposed. Hurting and hoping.

Her eyes were bleary from not getting enough sleep. She felt like a wreck, as if she'd been sucked inside a whirlpool and dumped back to the ground. No bruises on the outside...but her insides were black and blue and trembling.

Holden opened the door, wearing a white T-shirt and shorts that showed he worked out and had great legs. Cara pushed in front of him, beaming at her and Grace, saying, "You're here! You're here in my house! You and Grace and Lion and Minnie and Quigley are all here!"

Abby gazed at her, Holden, Minnie, Lion, Quigley, and Epic, and a flood of emotion welled up inside her, filling her, turning her into a puddle of feelings. Tears warmed her eyes, and she crouched to hug Cara. Cara's arms clasped her neck tightly, and Abby smelled her little-girl freshness.

"I wish you were my mom," Cara whispered, again.

Abby was losing count of the number of times Cara said that. Each time it broke her heart—because she hated it that Cara's real mother didn't treasure her the way she deserved. The way any child deserved. She wanted to answer, but if she said anything, she knew sobs of relief and this overload of emotion inside her would burst out. And she would cry and cry and cry the way she'd done every night for months after her parents' deaths. Crying against her pillow, so Grace would never know.

Until her tears had dried up, and she'd thrown out her mildewed pillow and sworn she would never cry like that again.

Instead of words, she hugged Cara again and kissed her on her cheek.

Minnie was meowing at her, scratching her bent knee, her way of saying, *"Me, me, me. Pay attention to me."*

Then Minnie climbed up her knee and was between her and Cara. For a second, Abby was hugging both of them, then just Minnie, who scrabbled her way up to Abby's shoulders, her nails pricking through the cotton of Abby's purple top until she got close enough for Abby to lower her chin and kiss the top of her head and say in a voice that kept cracking, "Thank God, you're okay. Thank God, thank God."

Quigley was meowing at her, and she laughed shakily and crouched to hug him, too. Grace was crying over Lion, telling him how much she'd missed him, and Lion was licking her face.

Then Epic was there, meowing to his friends, and Abby petted her then crawled on the rug to pet Lion.

Looping her eyes over Lion's neck, she felt Holden's gaze on her. She knew she looked like a crazy woman, but she didn't care.

This was what an open wound looked like, she thought, all the nerve ends exposed. That's what one night without her pets had done to her.

Leaning her forehead against the side of Lion's neck, she breathed in his dog scent and hung on. Movement came beside her. A new, citrusy scent added to the dog scent as a hand touched her back.

She turned just enough to see Holden, a concerned frown on his forehead. For a mad second, she fought an impulse to release Lion and fling herself against his broad shoulders.

"Here." He thrust two tissues at her.

She looked at him for a blank second before she realized tears were running down her cheeks. As if hypnotized, she took the tissues then wiped her eyes and blew her nose. She didn't know what to do with the used tissues, so she shoved them in her shorts' pocket.

"Thank you for calling," she said, her voice hoarse. "I don't know why they left my home, or why they came here."

"Neither do I, but I thank them for it."

She scrambled to her feet, and he straightened. They stood so close to one another she could see the navy blue flecks in his eyes that stared at her as if she were a chocolate cake and he was a chocoholic who'd missed his last Chocoholics Anonymous meeting.

"Remember what I said the first time you came to my house?" she asked.

"I remember *everything*," he said, his voice low and intimate.

Her quivering emotions took another leap. She shot him a look that said, *Don't do this to me.*

"I said I wanted to kick you."

The corners of his lips slanted up. "I appreciated your restraint."

"You shouldn't. I've thought of kicking you often since then. In fact, I'm thinking about kicking you right now."

"I like that about you."

"You *want* me to kick you?"

He shook his head, one side of his mouth curved up. "I find it refreshing that you're not like most women. You don't look at me and see a pile of money." He leaned forward, and when he spoke in a husky murmur, she could feel his warm breath on her face. "You see a man."

Heat poured through her. "A flawed man. You don't laugh enough."

"I know. I need someone to help me work on the flaws. Someone to make me laugh."

She stared at him and started to shake. The last thing she wanted right now was to cry in front of him. She snapped around. "I need air," she said, her voice wobbling.

She couldn't stay here. If she did, she would melt. She headed toward the French doors. The back of her neck prickled, and then the entire skin of her back joined in, and she glanced behind her, not surprised to see Holden. "Don't follow me. If you do, I really will kick you."

Then she opened the door, stepped onto the patio, and closed it behind her.

26

Holden looked behind him and saw Cara and Grace staring at him, their eyes wide and their mouths open. The dog and cats stared at him, too, then Minnie said something to him, and Quigley joined in. He had the insane idea they were urging him on.

"Stay," he ordered all of them. As if they would listen to him.

He opened the French door, stepped onto the patio. He was done with being fearful of the future. He was done with letting his past hold him back. He would fight for her love. He would fight for his chance at happiness.

Abby stood at the railing, her shoulders stiffening as he approached her. He hoped she really wouldn't kick him, but he wasn't going to let anything stop him from saying what he needed to say.

He halted next to her. A small breeze gusted, the sun shone down on them, the smell of the morning sunlight and dew drops on grass melded with the smell of water. He gazed at the lake. There were two fishing boats on the lake, one sailboat, and a couple in a two-person kayak.

"You like to kayak?" he asked. "Or sail or fish?"

"I kayak sometimes."

"If you lived here, you could kayak anytime you want."

"There's public access to the lake. I can already kayak anytime I want."

Laughter rumbled inside him. He loved it that she didn't fawn over him. Loved her sharp tongue. Loved her mind as much as he loved her body.

And he loved her body very much. He wished he could show her now, but they were on a patio with two young girls and four pets no doubt watching every move they made.

"I didn't kidnap your pets," he said. If one road to her heart wasn't working, then he'd try a different path. "We found them on the patio this morning."

"I know you would never kidnap them."

He gripped the patio railing to keep from putting his arm around her. He could tell by the tension radiating from her that she wasn't ready for it and didn't want it. Didn't want *him*.

Not yet. He needed to change that.

"Cara wants us to get together. I think Grace would like it, too." He looked at her, and she closed her eyes, her lips flattened into a line. He had the feeling she was on the verge of tears, teetering on a precipitous edge. He continued anyway. "Even our pets want us together."

She lowered her head and looked down at the grass. "I've never made any commitment to a man."

"Because of Grace?"

Still looking down, she shook her head. "At first, I wanted what my mom and dad had, and I couldn't settle for less. They...*loved* each other so deeply. I never felt that way about any boy or young man." She raised her head and glanced sideways with a small smile. "That goes for your brother."

"That's good. I would hate to be jealous of my younger brother."

She made a sound that was half chuckle, half sob. Then she put her hand over her mouth, as if holding back a cry. A half minute passed, and she lowered her hand and swallowed.

"After my parents died," she said, her voice low, "I used to say Grace was the reason. Because by that time, I'd learned that what my parents had was hard to come by."

"It wouldn't be less for me," he said.

She held out her hands and stepped back. "Please. Let me finish."

He faced her, curling his hands at his sides to keep from putting them on her shoulders and pulling her against him. "Go ahead."

"I think we're good for each other. You ground me."

"And you make me fly."

She gave another laugh with a cry in it, looked down, and then looked up. "When my parents were killed, it devastated me." She held up her hand again, and he bit back words of sympathy as she continued. "At nineteen, I thought I was tough. I thought I knew everything. But their loss was...heartbreaking. Horrible. I had to be strong for Grace but..."

"You don't have to be strong alone."

"But that's it. In the end, family and the people we care for, it's what matters most." Her eyes glittered with tears. "That night we made love—" She grimaced. "Had sex."

"Made love," he said.

She gave him a stern look. "Afterward, I thought maybe there was hope. That maybe I could love someone." She stopped and looked down then, her breaths harsh, looked up at him again. "I thought maybe I already had fallen in love... Just a little. And then..." She shrugged. "And then you couldn't wait to leave the next morning."

He groaned. "For the past two weeks you've been threatening to kick me. Go ahead and do it now. I deserve it for being so stupid."

"No, no, you were the smart one."

"I wanted to break my engagement before we went any further."

"You wanted a way out. No, no, don't shake your head. And don't be sorry. I'm glad for it. It happened so fast, and I don't blame you for wanting to slow it down. Last night, I walked for miles, looking for my three jail jumpers." She smiled faintly at his laugh before continuing, a frown scoring her forehead. "I was so worried for them. So many things could've happened, and I would never have seen them again."

"But they didn't happen."

"I know, but they could have. And the thought killed me. Though they're fine now, they will die sometime. And with every death, I'll...be hurt."

"So you'll never get another dog or cat again?"

She stared at him. "That's it. That's the real reason."

"Real reason for what?"

"For not settling with one man. I'm afraid you'll die, and I'll be alone again. That's why I was so ready to let you go."

"You—"

The door opened. "Daddy?"

He turned slowly, stifling a groan. "What is it?"

"It's her."

"Her?" He frowned.

Cara looked from him to Abby then back at him again. "You know. My mom. She said it's important."

"Tell her—"

Abby's hand on his shoulder stopped him. "That he'll be right there."

Biting her lower lip, Cara nodded and scampered away, the door closing behind her.

He swung back to Abby, and she was turning to the house. "Don't go."

"I have to take the pets back."

"Wait a few minutes. Please. I won't be long. I'll take the call, then we can talk in my office. Grace can watch Cara for a few minutes."

"I don't know. I—"

He leaned forward and kissed her. His arms around her, his mouth on hers, coaxing her to open her lips. Thinking it was now or never. Then his thoughts changed to *love me, love me, love me.*

Her mouth softened, and so did her body. Through the French door that hadn't shut all the way, he heard a giggle. He forced himself to pull back. Because if he didn't pull back now, he would be in big trouble.

Abby gave a husky laugh, shook her head. "Okay, okay, I'll wait for you." She hurried to the door, and he followed her, his steps deliberate as he thought of ways to convince her to give love a chance.

———

"You kissed Daddy," Cara said, looking up at her in the living room, her eyes shining.

The emotion Abby had felt before was back but different. The bitterness was gone, but the apprehension was there, the fear, the giddiness. But so were the want, the need, the hope. The thought that maybe this was it, after all.

The fear that maybe it wasn't it.

But his eyes...the way he'd looked at her...as if she was more delicious than the best ice cream he'd eaten, the best apple pie, the best cheese.

Or maybe it was her, looking at him. Smelling him. Tasting him. Wanting him.

She put her hands on her hot cheeks, aware that two girls and four animals were staring at her, waiting for her reply.

"Technically, he kissed me."

"You kissed him back," Grace said.

"I did." And it was good. Damn good. Or heavenly good. She wanted to do it again.

But that didn't mean anything except they were good together. Very, very, *very* good.

She bent and picked up Cara and twirled her. Cara giggled, and she giggled. When she put her down, she kissed her pets, saving Minnie for last, because she wanted to pet her the longest. She loved all her pets. They were all special. But Minnie was just a little more special. She was the one who sat in her lap the most, the one who'd given her the idea for the cat furniture. The one who was the smartest.

"Why did you leave?" she whispered. "Why?"

Minnie meowed and mewled and even said a few mrrwls before stopping, looking up at her, as if saying, *Your turn to talk.*

"Did you do this for a reason, huh?" She glanced up, and Cara was laughing at the way Quigley was sniffing her hair. "Did you do this to get me and Holden together?" Even as she spoke, she couldn't believe what she said.

Matchmaking cats. That was crazy.

Before she could take anything back, Minnie mewled and meowed and mrrwled again, as if replying. In the middle of a meow, Minnie stopped, looking at the hallway.

Her skin tingling, Abby followed Minnie's stare and saw Holden standing in the hall, tall and handsome, his jaw set in determination. The picture of a man no one would stop.

She stood, suddenly knowing she didn't want to stop him.

His eyes smoldered as she neared him. Behind her, Grace said, "Cara and I will play here, so don't worry about us. Take as long as you want."

"Brat," she said, not looking around, and Grace giggled.

Holden didn't smile or grin, but she saw the smile shining out of his eyes.

Hers, too. She felt the brightness, as if a piece of the sun lodged inside her. No wonder her body shook and heated, and with every step closer to him, she felt it shaking and heating more, her defenses weakening.

"In my office?" he asked.

She nodded, though there was something wrong with her because if he'd said in the bedroom, she would probably go with him. She would probably run into it and throw her clothes off then jump on him.

Inside his office, the first thing she noticed was his leather couch.

She turned to him. "Lock the door."

"Why?"

"So we can use the couch." She swept her hand at it. In case he didn't get her drift, she said, "To make love on it."

"You're ready to make a commitment?"

"I'm ready to make love." She held out her hands, the need clawing at her.

But instead of taking her hand and leading her to the couch, he remained planted in front of her. "I want to make love to you. But first I want the commitment. I love you. I want you. I don't want any other woman."

She stared at him, her arms dropping slowly to her sides.

He stared back. Standing solid. Like a mountain, she thought. Her mountain.

"You can't live in fear," he said.

"I've been living in fear for nine years." She tried to smile, and her lips wouldn't cooperate, so she talked again. "You helped me realize that. Being without Minnie, Quigley, and Lion overnight helped me realize that, too. The odds are that I'll outlive them. That I'll be hurt again. I'll cry buckets of tears, and then I'll have to go on with my life." Tears heated her eyes and thickened her voice. "But I'll never regret the time with them." She paused, taking in a deep breath. "And I'll never regret the time with you."

"So you do love me?" He stepped toward her.

"I'm crazy about you." She put her hand on his chest, as if that would hold him back. "And I feel crazy feeling so crazy. It's only been two weeks."

He still stared at her, and his eyes warmed, his lips smiling. It felt to her as if he were leaking love...and she leaked love right back. "When I met you ten years ago," he said, "I wanted to ask you out."

"Really?" She laughed breathlessly. "Why didn't you?"

"You'd been dating Ryan. I thought I wasn't your type. But you made me laugh."

"I made you laugh because I threatened to physically hurt your brother."

He grinned. "True. But my point is, it's not been two weeks. It's been ten years. Ten years is plenty long enough to fall in love."

Her heart beat fast. "Are you saying you love me?"

"Yes. I love you." He kissed her forehead, and this time she didn't try to hold him back. "I love you." He kissed her lips. "I love you."

Emotion swirled up inside her again, and this time, she put a name to it. Happiness. Pure happiness. Her doubts vanished like raindrops after a storm. "If you're crazy, then we're both crazy. I love you, too."

"How do you feel about being an instant mom? Juliana called to tell me she talked to her lawyer, and she's signing over custody of Cara to me." He frowned. "Will that be too much for you?"

"Too much? Are you kidding me?" Her voice rose. "I was an instant mom when I was nineteen."

"Do you regret it?"

"I regret my parents dying. I don't regret for one second that I've been acting as Grace's mom." She put her hand over his heart and felt the steady beat. With his news about Cara, the love inside her had grown. She felt it in her eyes, her throat, her heart, her belly, and even the soles of her feet. As if she had so much love inside her she could sprout wings and fly. "And I already love Cara. I won't regret it."

"I'll give you as much time as you need, but I want to marry you."

"Right away?"

"When you're ready. Let's not wait ten years again."

"I know what I want now." She frowned, because even with all the love inside her like a supercharged disco ball, she knew someday sadness would come. Someday, other people she cared for would die.

But not to love because of that? That wouldn't be a life; it would be a living death.

Still looking at him, she pulled his head down for another kiss. When this one was over, she felt wonderfully warm. "There's no need to wait," she said, her voice husky. "Two months? Would two months be too long?"

"I'd rather do this in two weeks," he murmured, wrapping his arms around her. "But I'll settle for two months. And you and Sam will be part of Eagleton

Furniture. We can drive to work together then."

"Your PR people will love that." She laughed. "Our marriage will make the partnership an even better story."

He bent his head to kiss her while she pushed up on her tiptoes and melted against him. When he pulled back from her, she moaned.

"I know you're worried that something will happen," he said, his voice low. "But my love will last. I will love you until my last breath. Until the last beat of my heart."

"I can do you one better. I'll love you *after* my last breath. I'll love you forever." She pulled out of his embrace, held out her hand for his, then drew him toward the couch. "And I'll make love to you now."

———

Minnie tipped her head up in the living room. The last she heard coming from Holden's office was their laughter then the creak of the couch. Since then, they'd gotten quiet. Very quiet. Except for the squeak, squeak, squeak of the couch.

A moan came to her ears, too quiet for Cara and Grace to hear as they played a game on the living room floor. It didn't sound like a moan of pain to Minnie; it sounded more like a happy moan.

What do you think they're doing together? Epic asked.

Can't you smell them? Lion asked. *They're mating.*

Minnie jumped on the couch in the middle of a splotch of warm sunlight. She, Quigley, and Lion had risked everything to get Abby and Holden together. She'd only slept in snatches last night, needing to be aware in case any owls or foxes came after them. And now...it was worth every minute of lost sleep and discomfort.

After all, she loved Mom and wanted her to be happy. Now Mom was.

Minnie closed her eyes. Her work was over, she was happy, Mom was happy, they'd never have to worry about losing their home again.

And now it was time to nap.

Save a Cat, Feed a Dog, Read a Book

25¢ from every HEARTS IN MOTION book sold will go to the Washington County Humane Society in Wisconsin.

Look for CHRISTMAS AT ANGEL LAKE, Rescued Hearts book 2—and more to come!

Acknowledgments

Thanks to Amy Remus, beta reader extraordinaire, and to my amazing editor, Amy Knupp at Blue Otter Editing. I sometimes agonize over finding the right name for my characters, so huge thanks to Beth Watson for naming her cat Quigley. As soon as I heard it, I knew I would use it in a story someday. My cousin, Nancy Lowell, fosters Siamese cats and generously shared information with me. Most of all, thanks to my sweet cat and a longer string of dogs for stealing my heart and sometimes trampling on it. I love every one of you.

About Edie Ramer

Edie Ramer is funnier on the page than in real life. A multiple award-winning writer, she writes stories with heart. She lives in southeastern Wisconsin with her husband, dog and one important cat.

In addition to her Rescued Hearts and Miracle Interrupted series, she's published in paranormal and sci fi romance, plus a humorous mystery. She's happy to be able to do what she loves nearly every day.